Going

Somewhere

TO

MURIEL DRAPER

Contents

GOING

SOMEWHERE

Paris

Pageantry

IN A ROCOCO ALCOVE ADJOINING the Duquesa's ballroom there sat in some discomfort a trio of *femmes du monde*.

"Do not dream of stopping at the Stuyvesant-Plaza. It sways, my dear, in the wind." With a traveler's air of authority Pisa Barteau gave the warning.

The seemingly scattered Princesse Angèle de Villefranche opened wide her avid eyes and said, "Is it possible?" Her eyes, having looked for fifty years on the dwindling aspect of her *milieu*, were turned in the direction of New York.

With a shrug which implied that her speculation was more authentic than fact, the Comtesse Fervante de Contrecoeur slightly squirmed on her marble bench. "I can't believe the architecture's careless," she announced. "Pisa must have stopped in a secondary hostelry. I'm sure the better ones are quite secure."

The Comtesse never overlooked an opportunity to pique Pisa Barteau. For this artist, whom she had known for many

(3)

years, had persistently refused to paint her portrait. The Comtesse had formerly been considered a very ravishing beauty. And as her beauty, almost her only asset, was now unquestionably waning, she feverishly sought its perpetuation in paint by distinguished artists. She resented the fact that Pisa Barteau had recently painted the Princesse de Villefranche. The Princesse at best had never been a beauty, and now, in the biased opinion of the Comtesse, her appearance was even fantastic.

But Pisa Barteau, with no eye for conventional "beauty," had found Angèle de Villefranche an absorbing subject. And her portrait, one of Barteau's best, was enjoying a forty years sojourn in the Luxembourg. It revealed the Princesse sitting in an avalanche of jet, her face turned toward a window which gave out on the pensive Forest of Fontainebleau. In her lap she clasped a lavender leather-bound copy of *Chéri*. And at her feet reclined a lazy, slightly cynical cat. The Princesse's enormous black eyes were bright and excited even on canvas. But around her mouth were lines engendered of careless, hopeful boredom. Her arresting face was rakishly imperious, combining the distinctive features of *grande dame* and *vivandière*.

"I may resort in the end to taking a *flat*," she said resignedly.

"Just when is it, Angèle, that you are sailing?"

"I'm off a week from now on the *Lethargic*."

"Ah no, that dreadful craft," sighed Pisa Barteau. "It rocks from side to side beyond belief."

"Pisa, now really," said the Comtesse de Contrecoeur, "there must be some disorder in your balance. On land and sea you seem to find life rocky."

For answer Pisa Barteau merely glared.

The Princesse looked as though all things were equally irrelevant. "I crossed to Egypt once and didn't mind it," she observed. "I went on a dahabeah up the—up the river there." It was characteristic of the Princesse's mind that it retained the word *dahabeah* while it failed to recollect *Nile*. "I'm all agog at going to America," she added, surveying vaguely a group of Duchesses who had just arrived in the ballroom.

"The Duchesse d'Èze now goes each year, and each time reports new wonders," said Pisa Barteau.

"Poor Cerise! She even reports new wonders in Dijon," the Comtesse sneered.

"I don't suggest she has discrimination," Pisa Barteau argued, "but still she is a hard one to surprise."

"I've never seen any advantage in surprises," replied the Comtesse. "I'm sure that in America life is one incessant 'Boo!'"

"That's it!" exclaimed the Princesse. "I hope that's what it is!"

"Angèle, after all . . ." The Comtesse was too weary to continue.

The adventurous Princesse Angèle de Villefranche, the resentful Comtesse Fervante de Contrecoeur, and the opulent portrait painter Pisa Barteau had retreated to the alcove less for the pleasure of conversation than for the major satisfaction of sitting. The ballroom was filling rapidly and chairs were at a premium. They sat, these three, for a moment in a state of silent enmity. For many years they had faced each other in one salon or another. Their early lively antagonisms were now worn down to a level line of lukewarm irritation. And the destination to which their quite impassioned decades had brought them was now the same salon in which they first had encountered each other. They were attending the Fall Fête of the Duquesa Barocca, the twentieth in succession which they had attended.

The life of the Duquesa Barocca had been a protracted costume ball. Her passion for masquerading had so augmented with the years that now it had become her sole preoccupation. Her years of concentrated effort to resemble nothing on earth had made her into something indeed unearthly. She had become, without having appeared on a stage, one of her century's greatest theatrical creations. Never following the mode in dress, the Duquesa made her most casual excursions into the streets in highly fanciful attire. The almost constant motif was concealment. Veils and flounces of lace were wont to cover her eyes and temples. Feathers from all the birds of the world made her ears lifelong enigmas. And the fur of all known animals served to guard from sight her chin. The world, on viewing the Duquesa, always said, "How young she looks!" Her face was well established in the consciousness of Christendom.

∽ PARIS PAGEANTRY ∽

It seldom occurred to anyone that for years almost no one had seen it.

To four a year the Duquesa now limited her balls: an annual Spring Fête in Rome, a Summer Fête in Venice, a Fall Fête in Paris, and a Winter Fête wherever she happened to be. Africa had been the scene of her last Winter Fête, an implausible affair at Mengo, at the court of the King of Uganda, whither the Duquesa had traveled by caravan in search of four Blacks to guard her bed. It was only in Uganda, the Duquesa had been told, that Blacks could be found with the somewhat exceptional physical qualifications that she in dream had particularly set her heart on . . .

A Ball at the Duquesa's seemed a species of hallucination to anyone attending for the first time. Few people however in recent years attended for the first time. They had all attended for years and years, and expected each year some new perverse excesses. Her audience disintegrating along with herself, the crescendo of the Duquesa's advance into realms of relative lunacy had thus far gone comparatively unnoticed.

This year, for her Fall Fête in Paris, the Duquesa had conceived a pageant depicting the Capitals of the World. "New York, though I've never seen it, is certainly the Capital now," she decided. And to represent New York became for thirteen weeks her problem.

Weeks in advance the Duquesa began constructive work on her costume. She had summoned a *couturier,* an engineer, a scene painter, a carpenter, and an electrician. "I want," she had advised them, "to make my entrance tower-ing as a skyscraper. I mean to burst forth all at once, a blind-ing edifice of bulbs." After eight weeks of work in progress the costume had attained such dimensions that work was no longer possible indoors. Not even the Duquesa's lofty ball-room would admit the mounting framework of wire, silver-cloth, rhinestones, and lamps. "From now on it will have to be continued in the park," she ordered. And the work went on in her garden under canvas. "This means the Fête itself will have to take place in the garden," reluctantly the Duquesa was forced to conclude. "Even though it will be November, a Fête *en plein air* is conceivable. At any rate it is not conceivable indoors if I can't get indoors with my costume," she reflected.

To precede her apparition she planned seven minor tableaux, choosing seven *femmes du monde* to represent the Capitals of the Past. After thoughtful elimination she had settled upon Rome, Carthage, Babylon, Sodom and Gomor-rah, Constantinople, Venice, and Monte-Carlo.

Having selected the cities and the ladies to represent them, the Duquesa had given *carte blanche* to these ladies in the matter of devising their respective spectacles. She was excited by the fact that Lady Rover, as Rome, was going to be thrown to a lion. The lion belonged to the Duquesa in whose bed it often slept. Indeed it was on quite friendly terms with Lady Rover as well, and no mishap was antici-pated when the two should meet in the tableau.

A gigantic roulette wheel was being built as a background for Madame Armada Menace as Monte-Carlo. She was going to come out, all strung with coins, and sing a page from the Gambling Scene of *Manon*.

Peter Bloomsbury and Aimée de Vaugirard had had no end of difficulty in devising something appropriate as the Cities of the Plain. Anything to do with the fate of Lot's Wife had been dismissed at once as far too obvious. They had finally settled on a ballet in the ultimate Diaghilev manner. "It's going to be something severe," Peter said. "Just blacks and grays and no shadows. We're going to make an entrance together, do some stylized German gymnastics, and then go sadly off—in opposite directions." The Duquesa was pleased by this conception, and said that it sounded very *chic*.

The pageant was scheduled for midnight, which now was not far off.

"I think I'll wander and see who's here." The Princesse de Villefranche rose from the edifice on which she had spent an hour. It was a fragile gilded bench supported by four groups of slender alabaster owls. "Sometimes there's someone new," she added as she tapped on the marble floor her foot which had been for some time asleep. Then, as though through a world of toys in which nobody ever grew up, the curious Princesse Angèle de Villefranche set out in the direction of the buffet.

"How ludicrous of Angèle to sail," the Comtesse de Contrecoeur whispered. "She seems to be in such thorough disorganization."

"Somehow she contrives to survive her havoc," marveled Pisa Barteau.

"Well, I feel that now she's setting sail, the worst is sure to happen." The Comtesse made her voice sound like a minor crack of doom.

Traversing the crowded ballroom toward the *buffet aux flambeaux* beyond, the Princesse de Villefranche was entertained within herself. "The fools," she mused, "they have no least conception of my project. They don't suspect that I am bent on *Memoirs*!"

The imminent voyage of the Princesse de Villefranche had caused wide speculation. "She has something up her sleeve," said many a Duchesse. And indeed she had, though to only a few had she divulged it. "Now that my age is fifty it is time for a change of scene." The Princesse had reached quite recently this conclusion. And a talk with the Duchesse d'Èze had convinced her that life must be sweet in New York.

"To have lived and not have known New York is like leaving life a spinster." The Duchesse d'Èze had said it with a fervor that was rare. ("Of that pathetic predicament, pray who is *she* to know?" had been the remark of Lady Rover on hearing the Duchesse quoted.)

To New York then the Princesse had booked a passage. "You're sure to come back crammed full of new impressions," the Duc de Tourbillon told her. And this remark had sown its seed in the fancy of the Princesse. "Why not put them down," she said to herself, "my store of new impressions? Most of my friends on coming back have done it."

The Princesse began to ruminate on the literature of Impressions. The Duchesse de Seine-et-Oise, for example, had spent three months in America, and on her return had written a book called *Où J'ai Perdu Mon Coeur*. André d'Assas had compiled a guide, *Ce Qu'il Faut Faire à New-York*. Puella Odéon had enriched the world with a work which bore an awkward appellation: *Les Choses Que J'ai Trouvées Les Plus Intéressantes En Visite Aux États-Unis*. ("Bah!" Lady Rover had harshly exclaimed on finishing reading this volume. "The things she found most interesting she hasn't ventured to mention.") A small book of verse had come from the pen of the old Duchesse d'Auteuil. *Des Souvenirs d'Acier* it was entitled.

> *"J'adore La Ville d'Acier—c'est belle,*
> *J'aime bien sa vie, sa vie cruelle . . ."*

"It seems that there is always room for another book of Impressions," the Princesse concluded. And she broached her project to the publisher of *Où J'ai Perdu Mon Coeur*. "I'm off to New York to amass some new impressions. I want you to sign me up," she put it to him.

Monsieur Oiseau was perturbed and dubious at first. And then he thought it over. "Though it is chaotic, Angèle de Villefranche does have a mind of her own," he considered. "She might conceivably turn out something unique." And apart from *belles-lettres,* the selling value of her name could not be ignored. No matter what were inside her book, her name would be on the cover. It would be the first book to bear, as its author's, the mighty name of Villefranche, an ancient name which symbolized French glory. In the end Monsieur Oiseau decided to risk it. And with the ministrations of a multitude of clerks, who retarded operations fanatically, the last female descendant of the line of Villefranche affixed her name to a contract. The transaction filled the Princesse with a gusto almost childish. "Perhaps I can penetrate precincts barely touched upon before," she said expansively. And on this note she had taken leave of her publisher.

As the Princesse gained the *buffet aux flambeaux* she was faced with the apparition of a creature quite ineffable. In a cloud of lace and gems galore stood Erika, Baronne de Bavière. The Baronne whose tiny feet had caused Pre-Raphaelites to sigh was now an anachronism which was lost but still at large. Imagining herself *féerie* forever, the Baronne had postured through gilded decades, and had emerged *sorcière,* unconscious of the change.

"Angèle, is that you?" cried the Baronne de Bavière. "My eyes are nearly *nil,* I'm so short-sighted."

"I'm hunting a glass," said Angèle de Villefranche. "My foot's quite asleep," she added. She stared disinterestedly at the Baronne who stood winding about her throat a piece of fur that seemed of length eternal.

∽ PARIS PAGEANTRY ∽

"I'm all worked up," said Erika de Bavière, "that I'm not appearing as München. Imagine something so *idiote* as not including München! Especially when she found room for such a *cul-de-sac* as Monte-Carlo. And Carthage even! Now where in the world is Carthage? I was planning to appear as Ludwig being drawn by a svelte black swan. In fact I was getting the wings and things fixed to fit Anthony Stowitts. Do you know Anthony? He's here somewhere—he's with me—but my eyes—I don't see him now. He's charming—English. But imagine, Angèle, don't you think it's *idiote* not to have me as München? I was going to make my entrance to the strains of the *Char-Freitags Zauber*."

"It's coming to, my foot," announced the Princesse. It was characteristic of Angèle de Villefranche that she entertained only one train of thought at a time. No matter what subject was on her mind it remained there until she dismissed it. And she never dismissed it until she was struck by something that seemed more diverting. The Baronne's garrulous confusion on the topics of München, swans, and Carthage did not affect the processes of the Princesse. If her foot were hurting she spoke of that. To her it seemed only sensible. The Baronne herself was likewise given to one-track mental functioning. And the two ladies seldom were able to enter into direct communication. They would face each other and conversationally wander down parallel paths.

"Something *tellement idiote*—" the Baronne was starting in to enlarge upon her subject when Anthony Stowitts crossed her line of vision and dissolved her train of thought.

He approached, a young Englishman of standardized good looks, and made his bow to the Princesse. "This boy is so nice," the Baronne introduced him. "He's a friend of Peter Bloomsbury," she added, winding her fur into something intricate.

The Princesse stared at him amiably and said, "I'm going to America next week."

Somewhat taken aback, Anthony Stowitts answered, "Really? On what ship?"

"The *Lethargic*. They say it's shaky."

"Funnily enough, I've a friend sailing on it too—from Southampton. I'm sure he'd adore to meet you. He's frightfully sweet. His name is Napier Knightsbridge."

"That's delightful," cried the Princesse. "I'm B–312. My foot's such a bore," she added quite engagingly.

Anthony Stowitts was disconcerted. "She's rather queer," he appraised the Princesse.

A gong announcing the pageant sounded, and the guests were thronging into the park. As they passed, the Baronne bowed only to those who were written about under different names in the work of Marcel Proust. To her such a mention was more impressive than inclusion in the *Almanac de Gotha*. The greatest disappointment of her life was that Proust had made no reference to her. She explained this away by saying that of course she was far too young.

"I say, it's started to snow!" exclaimed the Princesse.

"Then we must stay inside and find ourselves a window," said the Baronne. "We can look out at the pageant from the glass room where she keeps the stuffed panther."

Iokanaan, the Duquesa's pet among panthers, had died a theatrical death. In Amalfi one day she became suddenly aware that nothing in life was as beautiful as Iokanaan, and that even his beauty in time would tend to subside. Without further thought she then and there had shot him. *"Mourez parmi la voix terrible de l'amour!"* she had brought a line of Verlaine's *Sagesse* to bear on the occasion. Iokanaan, now stuffed, perpetually at his best, looked out to-night through glass eyes upon the Capitals of the Past. He stood on a slab of marble beneath a dome of glass.

Anthony Stowitts consulted his program engraved in gold on heavy vellum. "They're changing the order of events," he said. "They're starting with Monte-Carlo."

"Who is that—that horrible woman?" asked Erika de Bavière. Through her lorgnon she vaguely discerned the lines of Madame Armada Menace.

> *"Profitons bien de la jeunesse,*
> *Profitons bien du printemps . . ."*

As Madame Menace stood singing in gold-strung *décolletée,* snow fell gently into her hair. At last with a sweeping meaningless gesture she faded into the night.

"How absolutely awful!" said Erika de Bavière. "I don't think I ever heard anything so bad. I couldn't hear it at all," she made it worse.

"There's Lady Rover. What's she got on?"

"She's Rome. I guess it's a *toga.*"

"How lovely Alcibiades looks in that spotlight. His mane was curled especially."

"How *bête* to put Alcibiades in a Roman scene!" The Baronne at this could barely contain herself.

"Alcibiades, Erika, is the lion."

"I thought she named it Judas."

"The alligator's Judas," said the Princesse de Villefranche. She dropped the statement carelessly as if it were self-evident.

"What's this, Anthony?" asked the Baronne.

"Venice. Mlle. Puella Odéon."

"That dreary girl, what's she doing? I cannot see a thing."

"She's lying in a gondola."

"How vulgar! Who's that man bending over her?"

"He's the gondolier. It seems he is licentious."

"*Ah non, c'est trop fort,*" cried Erika de Bavière. "Imagine anything so crude and common. No gondolier would do such a thing."

"I've not found that the case," said Anthony Stowitts.

"What the case?" the Baronne raised her eyebrows.

"I mean to say that gondoliers, I've found, are often earthy."

The Princesse de Villefranche was silent, waiting impatiently for the final tableau. She was so excited by the thought of New York, and so curious to see how the Duquesa would represent it, that she regarded the preliminary tableaux with a petulant toleration. Even the ap-

(*16*)

pearance of the Cities of the Plain only half aroused her interest.

"Aimée looks quite a *femme damnée*!" exclaimed the Baronne, all eyes. "Oh look, she's jumping! How enchanting!"

"I had no idea Peter's leap was so good. I think he far outdoes Lifar." Anthony Stowitts was surprised by his rhyme.

"Which one of them is Gomorrah?" inquired the Princesse.

"The program doesn't say."

The alleys of the park, strewn with lighted blue bulbs, were now growing white with snow.

"Listen," said Anthony Stowitts, "someone is making an announcement." A stentorian voice was heard proclaiming that the Duquesa would make her appearance next, lest the storm should drive the guests indoors, and her tableau should be prevented.

The Princesse was breathless with anticipation. "'She's coming, her tent is tossing!" she exclaimed. Even the critical Baronne at this was moved to rise to her feet.

Something inside the Duquesa's tent began a forward motion. For a mighty minute Time stood still. And then the rest was darkness . . .

"Imagine!" wailed the Princesse, stunned with disappointment.

"Oh God in Heaven, help!" cried Erika de Bavière. Only the glass eyes of Iokanaan were visible in the darkness. The snow itself was falling now invisibly on the waste-land. Terrified by the light in the panther's eyes, the Baronne de Bavière set out quite blindly toward salvation, and the Princesse and Anthony Stowitts precariously followed.

"What happened?" cried Anthony, gaining at last the garden.

"She blew a fuse," replied an unrecognizable voice.

"She *what*?" asked the Baronne, still groping for the door.

"He says she blew the flues," relayed the Princesse, who had arrived out of doors and was stumbling down a formal garden path toward no very definite goal. Strange figures were scurrying in all directions, and the Princesse heard snatches of conversation from which she gleaned that the Duquesa had suffered a minor collapse from shock and rage, and that the lights would be out for hours.

Lady Rover materialized, carrying a jeweled flashlight and leading Alcibiades by the collar. "I'm taking this beast to the Crillon for safe keeping," she explained, drawing her toga into shape. In the light of Lady Rover's path the Princesse discerned Pisa Barteau and the Comtesse de Contrecoeur sitting seemingly hopelessly in the basin of an extinct fountain. Erika de Bavière was wandering wildly, apparently searching for Anthony Stowitts. The Princesse, rounding a curve in the path, found herself suddenly face to face with the Duchesse de Seine-et-Oise.

"I'm going home," the Princesse abruptly informed her.

"*I* can't," said the Duchesse de Seine-et-Oise. "I'm all got up as Carthage."

The Princesse prowled ahead and at last arrived at the gate which led to the street. "All got up as Carthage," she kept muttering to herself. She was disappointed and vexed, and it seemed to her suddenly that the Duquesa and her ball were as dead and remote as Carthage. Decidedly she was right, the Princesse reflected, in breaking away and going somewhere. The Duquesa was obsolete in her elaborate inefficiency, and her guests were all of them mummies.

"Mummies! Mummies!" grumbled the Princesse angrily, as she wandered alone through the streets of Passy in search of a passing cab. In America, she felt sure, things would be better regulated. There would be—well, what would there be? The Princesse was very hazy. She had been told, of course, not to expect to see cowboys, and had been warned that life in America was insane. But she had long ago accepted the fact that life everywhere was insane. She hoped at best to find in America a lunacy without cobwebs. "I'm sure that in New York the flues are trusty," she said aloud, and looking up she was startled to see that she had walked all the way to the Trocadéro.

LONDON

DEPARTURE

TAKING CARE TO PROTECT THE voluminous plaits encircling the waist of his trousers, Napier Knightsbridge knelt down and waywardly clicked a shilling into his fireplace.

"Within a week, thank God," he said, "I'll be beyond this primitive practice of warming up by the hour." He rose and brushed his hands as though they had come in touch with fuel.

Anthony Stowitts, back in London after a week of social duties in Paris, was seated on a steamer trunk, and the room was strewn with wardrobe. "In the Land of the Re-ed Hot Mammas," he began unpremeditatedly to sing, appropriating the tune of *From the Land of the Sky-Blue Water*.

"Don't sing about what you know nothing about," said Napier, turning to critically survey himself in a shaded full-length mirror. He was twenty-four, and handsome in the way that makes young Englishmen, when they are handsome at all, the handsomest young men in the world. It was not without reason that he found his reflection practically flawless.

The London flat he was vacating was a four-room and bath affair in the W.C. 1 section, which until her departure for Hollywood two years ago he had shared with his mother, Mrs. Pamela Woodley-Knightsbridge. After her victorious divorce from her husband (whom she had accused of numerous hushed-up things) Mrs. Woodley-Knightsbridge had been obliged to "make some money." She had resorted to teaching elocution, and had worked up a meager market when unforeseen good fortune came her way.

Miss April Overjoy, an "Emotional Queen of the Screen," on a vacation tour in England, was in sore need of vocal repairs. Inveterate chain-smoking for years in Hollywood had undermined her larynx. And just as she was approaching a state of complete inaudibility she was cast to play Paula Tanqueray in a talkie version of the drama. In despair she had gone abroad for a brief rest, and in London Mrs. Woodley-Knightsbridge was summoned to advise the panicky star.

"My dear," she informed her, "it's nothing serious. I can restore your voice in a month. You've let your vocal organ go so long, dear, you'll have to let me rectify your gutturals."

The star, without further thought, found a solution in suggesting that Mrs. Woodley-Knightsbridge should accompany her back to the Coast. It was just the culmination

Pamela had hoped for.

The association of star and coach proved to be mutually profitable. And April Overjoy won wide acclaim as Paula Tanqueray in the photoplay *Did She Do Right?*—her gutturals coming in for quite a lavish share of praise. After that Mrs. Woodley-Knightsbridge became a disciplinarian for other players. She gave counsel to former silent film stars who were now obliged to speak, and to former speaking stage stars who were now obliged to sing. And she became an invaluable authority in coaching casts to speak in Lonsdale comedies in the way that tradition has it that people in Lonsdale comedies speak.

It was during his mother's first season in Hollywood that Napier had "come out," as it were, in London. His greater freedom, occasioned by Pamela's absence, and his increased allowance from her augmented income, had facilitated his entrance into the outskirts of the *monde*.

Anthony Stowitts had directed Napier through various initiations, and had generally supervised his first season as a London *débutant*. Anthony's mission in life seemed to be moving in and out of drawing-rooms on some mysterious, urgent, futile errand. And this calling exercised on Napier a very strong appeal.

An epidemic of sailor parties had spread throughout that season. Everybody gave a party to which people came as sailors. For a week or so at the height of the vogue, tourists poking around through Chelsea and even Mayfair wondered what navy it was that was on such hilarious leave in

London. It was at Gala Jersey's sailor party that an important step was made in Napier's progress. When things were going very brightly, and everyone was singing chanties and having such a jolly good romp, Olympia Lunt was looking distinctly sour. "I'm mad," she said, collapsing on a couch. Why she was mad she seemed a bit too scattered to recall.

"Oh, oh, is our little *matelot* mad?" Peter Bloomsbury asked.

Overhearing these words none too accurately, Gala Jersey had cried, "Why, aren't we all? We're all of us *matelot*-mad!"

To Napier this remark indicated that an "amusing" song was in embryo. *Matelot Mad,* he mused, was really a most amusing title. He imagined himself writing a double-edged lyric, getting Bettina Wolsey to put a tune to it, singing it around at parties, taking it anon to a producer, and getting it into a revue.

"Funnily enough," he afterwards said, "it came about just like that." The song was interpolated in a revue called *Get Up and Rest,* and everybody sang it for a fortnight.

The lyric of the refrain which Olympia Lunt had un-wittingly sown the seed of, eventually in its finished form went as follows:

"I'm *matelot*-mad
To be *matelot*-had,
Though I'm dying to be good I guess I'm living to be bad,
'cause I've got that *matelot* madness now;
I'm *matelot-allured*

I never get inured,
Though it may be a disease, still I'm reluctant to be cured,
I've got that *matelot*-madness now!
I love to be around where lots of *matelots* abound,
So let me know if any ship of battle goes aground,
I rave about a *matelot,*
I crave a naval battle, oh
I'm absolutely *matelot*-mad!"

Pamela Woodley-Knightsbridge tried hard to market this piece as a theme-song in Hollywood, but after quite strenuous efforts she wrote disappointedly to Napier:

"Naps darling, I'm so sorry, but I simply cannot sell your song to the films. No one seems to be able to make head or tail of it. Our musical supervisor didn't even know what a *matelot* was. And when I told him, he said, 'Well, who the hell cares?' And then he went on and said that nobody would know what *inured* meant, and that as for the second line, it didn't mean a thing, and that as far as he could see, the lyric was *simply lousy*. Anyway, I am making my pupils use it, and perhaps I can drum up quite a sale. To-day I used it in Robert Reindeer's lesson. Probably you have seen him. He is billed as The Boy Friend Of All. We worked an hour on the last line of the lyric, and I quite wore myself out inducing him to put the *m* at the end of *I'm* instead of at the beginning of *absolutely*. He was delighted with my results and went away repeating the last line of the lyric over and over to himself. Of course, darling, I think the song is simply too frightfully clever. Only next time try to think up something a teeny bit less *precious*. All my love and kisses. Pamela."

But Napier did not develop further as a lyricist. He enjoyed stopping in at the Pavilion during the run of *Get Up and Rest*. And it was gratifying to read in the program:

"MATELOT MAD"
Words by Napier Knightsbridge—Music by Bettina Wolsey
Sung by BILLY MARVEL and YVONNE DÉBRIS

But while the whole thing was very amusing once, it would be a bore a second time, Napier thought. It proved in the end to be fortunate that Pamela had not disposed of the song in America. For *Get Up and Rest,* at the end of its London run, moved on to New York.

At the outset of Pamela's second season on the Coast, she was depressed to receive no raise in her weekly pay check. And she even had qualms concerning how long her position on the Coast would continue. "Eventually," she reflected, "the stars will all learn to know a vowel from a consonant. So, in case of a rainy day I really must start to pare the cheese."

❦LONDON DEPARTURE❧

First of all, she would give up the flat in London. What Napier would do without it she had not exactly decided. His earning capacity, of course, was acutely limited. But perhaps he could find a room somewhere, and find something steady to do. He must learn sometime to curb his extravagant, even *amphibious* tastes.

Mrs. Woodley-Knightsbridge was ruminating on the uphill problem of funds, when April Overjoy once again proved a source of manna. The star gave a dinner for some traveling Belgian royalty, and afterward she showed her guests into what she called her "chamber of horrors." It was a narrow parlor in which April, as her hobby, was collecting horrific pieces of Victorian furniture, *bibelots,* and unlikely prints.

Pamela's mind worked fast. "April, it's divine, this room, it's simply inspired!" she exclaimed. "The next time you're in London I can show you where to get some nightmares. I know of one sofa so hideous it would make your hair stand up on end."

"Is it really a fright?" Miss Overjoy was breathless.

"Oh heaven, *but an ogre*! Stuffed fit to kill, and upholstered in plaid, with woodwork, my dear, of a kind that halfwits dream of. Oh April, you ought to have it—it's of a *mauvais gout* supreme."

"I must have it," declared the star. "I'm out to get the world's best *movie goo.*"

"Oh, but it belongs to—to Lady Rover," said Pamela, still thinking fast. "I dare say she would not surrender it."

(27)

"Oh dear," wailed the star, "if she only would, I'd offer almost anything. What do you suppose she'd take?"

"Well, I'd offer three hundred pounds, darling. I'm sure she would never forego that sofa for a sum that sounded frittering."

"I'll write you a check for a hundred pounds in advance to egg her on," said April. And they then repaired to the Russian Room to drink some Turkish coffee.

Later that night Pamela wrote to her son:

"Dear Naps— When the lease is up in November I want you to give up the flat. Your mamma has got to begin to *conserve*. Put the goods in storage like an angel—all but the old plaid sofa. I have sold it to April Overjoy, so please have it packed and shipped at once. I'm enclosing a check for a hundred pounds, an advance I received on the sofa. And Naps, when you ship it, look up Lady Rover's address and use it as the return address. I told a tiny fib and said it belonged to Lady Rover. Of course I didn't want to appear as if *I* were trying to unload old junk. And the word *Lady* works on people out here like a spell—the darling sillies. So forgive your mamma, and see how long you can make the hundred stretch. It ought to last you quite a while if you're not too frightfully vicious. Love. Pamela."

Napier received his mother's communication in September, when he was deeply depressed over being alone in London. There was no one—*not a soul*—in town. Everyone had scattered along the French Riviera, and no one showed any intention of coming back to London early. Napier Knightsbridge, on account of meager funds had remained in town all summer. In postcards he sent to his friends he used what amounted to almost a fixed form message: "Darling, it is sizzling. I'm spending my summer simply sitting in cinemas. Sincerely. Naps."

With the arrival of his mother's letter enclosing the hundred pounds, the world looked suddenly brighter to Napier Knightsbridge. He was dying to go somewhere. He would give up the flat, buy some new clothes, and take a ship to New York. New York seemed far more glamorous to him than the South of France. And having made this decision, he ceased to envy his friends their travels.

He found he had quite a number of reasons for wanting a change of scene. The London summer had been boring, and the prospect of the coming season was bleak. London without the Russian Ballet seemed about as deadly as Bayreuth without festivals. People too were rapidly vanishing off the local scene. Anthony Stowitts, in the interests of health, was going to Cairo for Christmas, and was planning to spend the rest of the winter in the tracks of Gide in Algiers. Everyone else was flocking to Paris where flats were decidedly cheaper. There was nothing "amusing" looming in London. The Sitwells were not engaged in teapot tempests with anybody. There were no exciting new Negroes announced for the *Café de Paris*. Neither comedy, tragedy, revue, operetta, oratorio, cantata, nor masque was promised by Noel Coward. Everybody was sick to death of going to parties as sailors. People had become converted to talkies and were even considering marriage. Nobody seemed to be feeling as sportively post-war as before, and more and more eyes were turning admiringly in the direction of the Princess Elizabeth.

Convincing as these reasons for leaving London appeared to Napier, they would scarcely appear equally persuasive to Pamela. "No Ballet? Why, Naps," she would be sure to reply, "there's no Ballet in New York either." And so on she would go throughout the other reasons. So Napier exercised selection in presenting his mother with his plan:

"Dear Pamela, how simply ripping about the sofa! I'm dying to know what you got for it if the hundred pounds were only an advance. The packers said I was crazy to ship it—that it wasn't worth the wood it took to crate it. But I was clever and said it was an *heirloom*. Billy Marvel said it was absurd for me to pay shipping costs because he could arrange to have the sofa shipped to New York with the props of *Get Up and Rest* for nothing, if only, he said, there would be someone to look after it in New York and ship it on out from there. So I am going across to New York to do this. My passage is not much more than the shipping costs would have been if I'd paid insurance and all

that. Besides it would be very ticklish trying to put
Lady Rover's address on all those millions of things
you have to sign. They would be sure to send her some
receipt or something, and people say she's a glutton
for going to court. When I get to New York I can use
her name without any risk.

I'm dying to go to America, darling, on account of
the *opportunities*. England doesn't hold much for anyone my age, and I'm dying to sort of *get on*. I hope
you won't be cross, for this move means a saving *in
the end*. I'll not leave until November when the lease
will have expired. Good-by. Naps."

Napier awaited with mild anxiety the reactions of his
mother. Weeks passed, and when finally he received her
letter it was plain she had not received his. For hers, a
very surprising document, was postmarked Honolulu:

"Dear Naps— Here I am in Hawaii, of all places,
and on my way to still remoter islands. We're at work
on *Lithe Limbs,* starring Robert Reindeer, a South Sea
scenario with Dulcy Wee as nothing but *female support*. Poor dear, she went three pounds beyond the
limit her star contract permitted, so now they have
reduced her to being a leading woman. Robert's rôle is
that of a native pearl diver who turns out to be the son
of a flighty English peeress. And since I had to come
on to coach him to speak with a *soupçon* of authentic

British delivery, they asked me if I thought that I could possibly play the peeress. I needn't tell you that I have *jumped* at the chance.

The undersea scenes are quite enchanting, and some days I get into an outfit and go down to the bottom and look on. Things are going better for your mamma, darling. And, thinking it over, I've decided not to have you give up the flat after all. More soon. Pamela.

P. S. It's divine here."

This letter, arriving three days before his departure on the *Lethargic,* was something that nothing could be done about, Napier concluded. "It's just one of those things," he said resignedly. And the day before sailing he dashed off a final note to his mother:

"Dear Pamela—When you get this I will be across the pond. I don't know where I'll stay in New York, but you can always reach me in care of *Get Up and Rest.* I'm down to fifty pounds in case you want to be an angel. Love and kisses. Naps.

P. S. What an awfully funny life you seem to be leading."

Late that afternoon Anthony Stowitts had come in to help him pack, and had been very sweet for an hour or two, and had sat and watched him pack. Anthony was full of diverting gossip about the Duquesa Barocca's ball, and he wrote a note of introduction for Napier to present to

∾ LONDON DEPARTURE ∾

the Princesse de Villefranche on the ship. He warned him that the Princesse was rather odd, but that she was nevertheless a sweet old sport.

Though Napier was sailing to America with only fifty pounds, he felt that on his last night in London he must dine at Strapontin's. This restaurant was referred to as *London's new oasis of chic*. "How virile Marie's work is growing!" Lady Rover had exclaimed the first time she laid her eyes on the murals in the bar. But the work was not by Laurencin, though it did bear affinitive earmarks which might easily have confused a *connoisseur* more sensitive than Lady Rover. Above the bar a mural stretched, disclosing a dozen pale azure ladies grouped in a hazy mountain scene, engaged in letting their fingers roam the throats of ivory horses, or carelessly plucking at mandolins, or vaguely contemplating lilies. A smaller decoration on the adjoining wall showed a mauve young woman with raven eyes intensely regarding a pear.

In the bar Napier and Anthony were surprised to find Peter Bloomsbury and Aimée de Vaugirard. They were standing up imbibing Bitter Campari. All four cried "Darling!" and "Angel!" and Aimée de Vaugirard said "Bless you!" She went on to add, "We're such wrecks, my dear, we've just this minute flown across the Channel. We came over for a *Squab à la Strapontin*."

"What are you doing later on?" asked Anthony. "We might join up at Armada Menace's recital."

(33)

"My dear, we can't," said Aimée. "We're flying back to Paris the minute we've dined. We have a date with some Toulon sailors to go to the Rue de Lappe. And you know the Rue de Lappe closes early. But I'm flying back over here to-morrow and we might go somewhere then. I'm coming over to tea with Lady Rover. She's laid up, poor dear, with some infection she caught from Alcibiades, the lamb."

"What lamb?" Napier was mystified.

"Oh, not a *lamb* at all, actually, darling. I forgot you didn't know. It's a lion—but almost always such a lamb. It seems the commotion of the Duquesa's pageant riled him. And when Lady Rover set out to take him to the Crillon overnight, he chose—the scamp—to bite her in the taxi."

"Not really, Aimée?"

"My dear, she's on the verge of amputation."

"How *awful*! I must send her a plant."

"Oh do be an angel and do."

Aimée de Vaugirard then selected a table on which stood a Lalique bowl of bright brass tulips and tin sweet peas. And sitting down she was pleased to find herself facing a Chirico, wherein a lithe voluptuous horse and a rather squat Greek temple were seen surprisingly juxtaposed in a shuttered light green bedroom. "I must try to get a facsimile of that painting," Aimée mused. "It makes me feel so excitedly haphazard."

Aimée de Vaugirard's life had been spent in haphazardly joining movements—so consistently haphazardly that it approached being systematic. She had been an excited dev-

∾ LONDON DEPARTURE ∾

otee of no less than a dozen *ismes*. A *Dadaiste* in her teens, she had turned *Sur-Réaliste* in her twenties. For two years she had said nightly prayers to a statuette of Josephine Baker. Then eventually finding emptiness even in Ethiopia, she had fastened her faith to Rome. But she still felt lost, and now at thirty she was planning to become a Nudist. She wanted to integrate her life in a process of simplification. And after all, she concluded, nothing in her life was "really tangible" except her body. . .

Resisting reverie reluctantly, she turned to Napier and smiled. "It's lovely to be with you your last night in London. But Peter and I are such wrecks, my dear, I hope you won't think we're dumpy. But we had such a night last night in the *boîtes*."

"Oh Aimée, how could you face it?" Anthony Stowitts had said good-by to *boîtes* and all that at twenty.

"My dear, we looked in at *La Lettre à Maritain,* a chic new little Neo-Catholic bar. It's smart and severe, done up like a cloister, and the only thing they serve is Benedictine."

"You have to buy a quart," Peter added.

Napier's attention had wandered to focus on a husky, obviously American, young woman who was seated at a near-by table. "What an amazing girl," he exclaimed. "I just overheard her say that she was going to swim to Belgium or something."

Anthony Stowitts was ready, as always, with accurate illumination. "It's Winona Outing, the Wisconsin Wonder. She hopes to succeed to-morrow as the first American female

(35)

to swim the Channel breast stroke in November."

"Hasn't almost everyone done that?" inquired Aimée.

"No. Americans have done it, but never in November. And it has been done in November, but not with the breast stroke. An Argentine did it once with the breast stroke, but was by no means a female. So Miss Outing stands a chance to win the title."

Aimée de Vaugirard looked amazed, and then she said, "How priceless!"

A bus passing by on its way to Wapping bore along a flamboyant message: "AT QUEEN'S HALL TO-NIGHT—MADAME ARMADA MENACE IN HER FINAL CONCERT APPEARANCE IN THE FLESH."

"I'd like to have gone to that recital," said Anthony. "It's apt to be an event. You know Madame Menace has some plan for canning her singing in America. She's going over there on some fearful project."

"It's very sensible of her," Aimée commented. "Her audience always upsets her, but she really can sing when she's alone."

At this moment Gala Jersey entered the restaurant, highly excited and breathless. "My dears," she cried, "I've just come from Queen's Hall. Armada Menace couldn't sing a note. She came out and just stood there petrified."

Madame Menace, it seemed, had suffered such panic at the thought of her public farewell in the flesh, that once on the platform she had gone all to pieces, and had run to the wings *in a state*. Bemoaning her chronic stage-fright

(36)

she had sobbed aloud, *"C'est plus fort que moi. . ."* (And her accompanist, pacing the wings, overheard her and perplexedly said to himself, "How odd of her to warm up on Mélisande.") After a further unsuccessful attempt to perform the aria from *Carmen, Je dis que rien ne m'épouvante,* apologies had at last been made for Madame Menace's indisposition, and money had been refunded at the box-office.

"Poor dear, *quel dommage,*" said Aimée, amused.

"Farewells to the flesh are always apt, I've found, to be *fiascos,*" Anthony observed.

"Well, anyway," Gala Jersey went on, "I was glad to get away early, for I've still some packing to do. I'm going to America again to-morrow. But not on the *Lethargic,* Naps. I'm on the *Anglomania* because the jazz-band's colored." Gala Jersey had an intense predilection for people of bister pigmentation. She was a disarmingly likeable girl with lapis lazuli eyes, whose frequent sensational excursions into the realm of the tender passion were always overlooked by her friends who would say, "Gala is frightfully indiscreet, but after all she does know a lot about old editions." Her intimate knowledge of folios and illuminated letters made up in their estimation for her lack of experience in the field of conventional virtue.

"Are you going to America in the rôle of traveling saleswoman again?" Anthony asked her.

"Of course, such a bore, but I've got three treasures to sell over there on commission—an old Chaucer, an old Benvenuto Cellini, and ten manuscript pages of Proust.

Olympia Lunt has given me a letter of introduction to a sculptress named Lanslide she knows in New York, who will be sure to buy the Cellini. She says she's a Crœsus who sculpts on the side, but is really the most divine bum."

"Olympia gave me a note to her too," said Napier.

"And what are *you* going over to sell?" Gala Jersey inquired of Napier. She was firmly entrenched in the concept that no young Britisher ever went to America unless he had something to dispose of.

"Only a sofa," Napier started to say, but he changed it to "Only my soul."

"I think it's rather weird of Naps to just set out like this," said Gala to Anthony. "I wonder whether in America he'll be equipped to stand the gaff." Gala would have been perplexed if pressed to define "the gaff," or to say with what equipment a man best stood it. Her vocabulary was altering strangely under the strain of gangster talkies.

"Naps will get on," said Anthony. "He has a supernal profile, and a figure too, though he sort of lets it slide. He doesn't dope, and he has a thoroughgoing Diaghilev-period background. He isn't equipped to cope with anything, but what is there for him to cope with? There's nothing to do but just get by, and Naps is sure to do that."

"Of course he is," said Aimée. "And now, Peter, we must fly. It's getting later than late."

Checks were paid, and Peter and Aimée hurried away to Croydon. "I hope my pilot hasn't gone and fuddled himself with stout," said Aimée in parting. She added no very

(38)

sweeping good-bys. She was flying back to-morrow.

Gala Jersey was reinforcing two delicate arc lines on her forehead half an inch above the level of her eradicated eyebrows. "I do think, Naps, you'd be more sensible to stay here and go on the dole," she said.

"I may do that later," Napier smiled. "But something, I don't know what it is, makes me want to go somewhere first."

"You know perfectly well what it is," Anthony yawned. "It's just the Decline of the West."

"Don't be so pre-Waugh," said Gala Jersey. "The whole West isn't declining. It's only the White Race that's giving out. The Blacks are going to consume us." Her inflection carried overtones of the ecstasy of submission.

Napier Knightsbridge felt apprehensive as they filed out into the fog.

TRANSATLANTIC

EPISODES

THE *LETHARGIC* LAY IN THE
Southampton harbor, looking reluctant to pull out. Napier
saw his baggage swung on board and went down to investigate his cabin. Unable to afford a first-class passage, he
had insisted on traveling second-class against the advice of
his friends who urged him to travel third. In November,
they said, the second-class would be filled with bearded im-
migrants who avoided going third-class in order to escape
something tiresome at Ellis Island. Napier never understood
these things. The second-class, he argued, was obviously
that much better than third, and certainly it did not sound
so pauperish. The agent who sold him his passage told him
he was putting him in a room for three, but that undoubtedly, in November, he would have the room to himself.

This did not prove to be true. As Napier entered the
stateroom he was faced by two rabbis, who looked about
eighty years old, their faces cracked like crêpe paper, and
their eyes sunk into pits. In flowing black robes or figured

(41)

silk they were opening paper bundles. Both of them spoke incessantly in high, cracked voices. In the washbowl they had placed a bouquet of red roses, and they were now engaged in arranging a row of pineapples under the berths.

Napier's heart sank. What was he to do—spend seven days and nights in a cabin with these old ghosts? He felt that he could not cope with it, and he went to the purser to complain. The purser agreed that it was a most unfortunate juxtaposition, and suggested that something might be done about switching him into a cabin with someone less objectionable than the rabbis. He told him to come around again at midnight. By that time things would be squared away, and some improvement could undoubtedly be made.

Napier put in a restless day and returned to the purser at midnight. "Got you all fixed up," the purser said, "you can move into D–400. There's only one other occupant. A nice young fellow, an American who has won some prize or other."

The young American, no matter how bad, could not be worse than the rabbis, reflected Napier as he entered D–400. On the floor of the stateroom sat a dark-haired young giant surrounded by magazines. He was stripped to the waist, and as Napier came in he smiled in a friendly fashion. His smile was of a kind Napier had never seen except in tooth-paste advertisements.

"Am I disturbing you—moving in like this?" Napier asked.

"Not at all, old man, come right on in. They told me

someone was coming."

"I'm sorry—bursting in like this—but I've just been switched from a den of roses and pineapples and rabbis."

This surprising statement did not appear to surprise the young man at all. His attention was directed only to the problem of Napier's luggage. "Here, old man, let me give you a lift," he said, hoisting a suitcase to a shelf. He picked it up like a feather and deposited it with a theatrical muscular flourish. The muscles of his back and shoulders were magnificent. He even seemed to pose for a second before he dropped the bag.

"I see your name is Knightsbridge, old man. I'm mighty glad to meet you." He took Napier's hand in a grip so firm it was agony. "Zukor's my name," he added. "Victor Zukor. Just call me Victor."

In view of this statement Napier was surprised to see emblazoned on the young man's luggage the somewhat sweeping cognomen: MR. AMERICA.

Victor Zukor's eyes followed Napier's as they focused on this title. "My real name's Zukor, but on this trip I'm known as Mr. America. I won the title last summer at Asbury Park."

"I see," said Napier, understanding nothing.

Victor Zukor sank with a bound to the floor to pick up his magazines. Napier noted that they were in several languages, all of them profusely illustrated: the German *Querschnitt, Sport und Sonne,* and *Schönheit;* the British *Health and Strength;* the Scandinavian *Gymn* and *Swing;* the

French *Sport et Santé;* and a sheet called *La Suisse Sportive*.

"Look here, old man, here I am in this Swedish paper," said Victor Zukor, pointing to his picture posed as the Apoxymenus of Lysippus. "Why, man alive," he added, "I'm coming out in everything." He brought, one by one, to Napier's attention the astonishing number of magazine reproductions of his photographs, nearly all of them nudes. "Just look at that *serratus magnus,*" he beamed. "That's what made me Mr. America."

Napier agreed that it was "too extraordinary," but he was still in the dark as to how it made him Mr. America. Pressed for an explanation, Victor Zukor divulged some data. With interest decreasing in the contests in which a Bathing Beauty each year became Miss America (or ultimately Miss Universe), an enterprising publication which went by the name of *Muscle* had sponsored, two years ago, a similar contest for men, which had taken place at Niagara Falls. From all parts of the country, Victor Zukor explained, had come track-runners, weight-lifters, pole-vaulters, discus-throwers, adagio dancers, life-guards, and models to compete for the proffered title. There had been some unpleasantness over its award because Mr. Hot Springs and Mr. Ann Arbor had tied in the judges' decision. It was finally settled by giving Mr. Ann Arbor the title Mr. East of the Mississippi.

The interest in this contest had been surprisingly widespread, and was more than doubled the second year when it was held at Asbury Park. In addition to the title of Mr. America, the winner was to be given a three months trip to Europe under the auspices of *Muscle*. Victor Zukor who competed as Mr. Poughkeepsie was awarded the title without any hitches.

His trip to Europe had been a prolonged celebration of Victor Zukor's physique. In Athens he had been fêted on the Acropolis. He was photographed in Sparta and on the shores of the Hellespont. In Rome he received a welcoming reception in the ruins of the Baths of Diocletian, and the straggling little *bagni* along the Tiber were given over for a week to carnival. But the greatest ovation of all had been held in store for him at Berlin. A frenzy was what he said that city went into. A parade from the Wannsee to the Brandenburger Tor had been organized, and Victor Zukor had led it, wearing a zebra-skin *cache-sexe*, a gift from the Berlin branch office of *Muscle*. The parade broke up with a picture being taken at the foot of a statue of Bismarck.

His tour officially over, Victor Zukor had been offered a first-class passage back to the States or an unofficial week in Paris with a second-class passage back. He had chosen the latter and now he felt he had made a minor mistake. Paris had taken little note of his presence, and he had spent his days in the Louvre alone, studying poses of secondary deities. He already knew by heart all the poses of the first rank gods.

It was one o'clock when he finished his story and he said he must go straight to bed. Napier was avid for further facts concerning his European tour. What for instance did he think of life as lived along the Kurfürstendamm? Victor Zukor inferred that this was a river, and said he had never been near it. And he really had to go straight to bed because it was already past his limit.

Napier was unable to destroy Victor Zukor's determination. With an agile gesture Mr. America swung himself into the upper berth. In less than five minutes his regular breathing revealed that he was fast asleep.

Napier had scarcely gone to sleep when he was abruptly awakened. It was morning, and Victor Zukor was naked, touching the floor with his fingers for the hundred and fiftieth time. "Hurry up, old man, or you'll miss breakfast. It's after eight o'clock."

Napier said he would ring for some toast and coffee in bed.

"Go on," said Victor Zukor. "Don't you want to radiate power?"

"Want to what?" asked Napier who was still only half awake.

"I said, don't you want to reap glowing rewards and learn to radiate power?"

Napier, reviewing his vocabulary, found he had nothing to reply.

Victor Zukor was lifting one arm against the pressure of the other. "You've got to give Nature a chance," he said, "or you'll be a human cipher. If you don't do any building up, what will She think of you?"

"What will who think of me?"

"The girl of your dreams."

Napier, amused, again had no answer. "How can you do all that before coffee?" he asked through a yawn.

"Before *coffee*? Say, pal, I never touch it." He went on with his strenuous flexing. "Do you see what I'm doing? I'm using the system of Aggressive Self-Resistance. It's better than apparatus. All you've got to do is simply learn to resist yourself."

The ship was swaying slightly, but Victor Zukor was firmly on his feet. He was now doing the "stiff-legged pick-up" which he said helped the ham-string muscles. "Feel my *gluteus minimus*," he ordered. "The best way to develop that muscle is to get someone else and do a mutual. Pull up that chair and we'll do some resistant leg-work."

But Napier said he would do nothing of the sort before he had breakfast.

"You're sure a shilly-shallier," said Victor. "But I'll develop your grit and gumption by degrees," he added good-naturedly. They dressed and went into the dining room and ate some hot cereal and eggs. Across the table sat the rabbis, mournfully munching pineapples. Most of the other passengers were grizzlies.

After breakfast Napier went up to the first-class quarters to deliver his note of introduction to the Princesse de Villefranche. He consulted a list of the first-class passengers to see what cabin the Princesse was occupying. In glancing through the list he looked for other well-known names. Celebrities were always trooping to America in November.

But they did not seem to be numerous on this crossing of the *Lethargic*.

The first name Napier recognized was that of Madame Armada Menace. "She's lost no time getting out of England," he said to himself in passing. Farther down he saw the familiar name of Mr. Wilburton Renegade, an American publisher with a branch in London, who since the success of *Queen Victoria* had published practically nothing but intimate biographies. The Princesse de Villefranche, he read, was in B–312. At the end of the list a name struck Napier as being extremely curious. Alphabetically, the last of the first-class passengers was Mrs. Niobe Why.

He called a boy and asked him to deliver his note from Anthony to the Princesse. He then returned to his stateroom, hoping to receive a prompt reply.

The boy, before knocking at the Princesse's door, gave his uniform a tug and a pat. This was only his second trip across, and his first look at royalty was imminent.

"Come in," two women's voices answered his knock.

Opening the door, the boy was startled by the sight which met his eyes. The Princesse was on her hands and knees, looking highly disorganized. She was wearing a voluminous bathrobe of flowered Turkish toweling. Her maid, Mirabelle, a wild-eyed wench, was also on her hands and knees.

"We're looking for *Albertine Disparue*," said the Princesse in a desperate voice. As she spoke she tossed her head

(48)

to shake her graying hair from her eyes.

"Not the book, the cat," said Mirabelle, who thought this made things clearer.

The Princesse was taking her cat to America against the advice of her friends. As a kitten its chief characteristic had been a desire to stay out of sight. The Princesse's rambling apartment in Paris had provided her cat with superb opportunities for indulgence of its whim. Often for days she would never see it at all. And this deprivation seemed in some way to delight her. She had named the cat *Albertine Disparue* after the volume which had just appeared. Only recently she had taken to calling it Albertine for short.

"I've brought a note for you, Madame," said the boy.

"Can't you help?" said the Princesse, addressing the boy, but looking under the bed.

"Where shall I put it?" he asked, indicating the note.

"Wait until we find it first. We'll put it on my pillow."

The boy put the note on the pillow and went away confused. The Princesse said, "Fancy that boy coming in!" and once more looked under the bed.

Mirabelle had gone into the adjoining room, pursuing a clew of her own. "I've found Albertine," she called to the Princesse. "I had locked her in a wardrobe trunk."

The Princesse got up and scrutinized them both and broke out in a roguish laugh. "I'll soon have to call the two of you Plum and Sweet Cheat Gone," she said.

The cat, a long haired, dark gray Persian, started in to pull Mirabelle's hair. The Princesse watched this activity intently and said, "I must look for my deck chair."

She put on a black wrap which was lined down the front with a row of diamond shaped buttons, and set out in quest of her chair. On the way she passed the shuttered windows of the *Lethargic's* Royal Suite. She had sought to engage these rooms herself, but they had been booked for weeks in advance by an American family named Basch. The Princesse smiled as she wondered whether this suite contained a throne.

She settled down in her deck chair and tucked the robe about her knees. The day was bright and the sea was smooth, and the Princesse took in a long deep breath as she focused a friendly gull.

The seeming precariousness of the Princesse's mind was due to her conception of time. She lived exclusively and intensively in the very immediate present. The past, even the past of five minutes ago was for her something finished and forgotten. And the future was something far away with which she established no connection. She attended to the nearest matter at hand, no matter how trivial it was. If she found herself faced with two matters at hand, she selected the more insignificant. Insignificance, she found, was almost always charming and delightful.

As a girl the Princesse had never fitted in with her lofty surroundings. In Paris in the *temps des équipages* she was bored by driving in carriages. She would drive up the Champs-Élysées in state because it was expected of her. But then she would order her *cocher* to drive on to a rollicking fair at Neuilly. Here she would shoot at marks and look in on framed-up wrestling matches. Later on she was the first French *femme du monde* to buy an electric buggy.

In her tastes in art the Princesse again diverged from her Faubourg's standards. She would yawn at the Comédie Française and walk out on *Andromaque*. As relief, she would escape to a music-hall and admire La Belle Otero. The Princesse Angèle de Villefranche had little sympathy with the grand manner.

Her love affairs had been minor escapades of no importance. After one first disappointment she had taken leave of the major emotions. Could the events of her life have been displayed, they would have formed a line-up of *bibelots*. A well-made old shoe in the Musée de Cluny gave her greater pleasure than the entire façade of Notre Dame. In a *lavabo*, if she saw a card reading, *"N'oubliez pas vos bagues,"* she would find this document so diverting that she would promptly forget her rings. The Princesse's friends were never wont to take her very seriously. She never resented this, for their attitude fitted in with her own conception.

The war had caused a temporary lapse in the Princesse's frivolities. She had been deeply moved by the suffering she saw, and had done all she could to relieve it. But once it was over, she saw the war in a very different light. If such a colossal world-wide tragedy ended up in such feeble farce, it seemed to the Princesse it were wiser to take one's farce without the tragedy. She returned with renewed animation to her former preoccupations, concentrating on *Bals Mu-*

settes and various other less regal pursuits. . .

In the chairs at her right on the *Lethargic* deck sat a man and woman and a child about five years old. The child had a dimpled baby face that bore signs of being rouged, and her hair which emerged from a velvet toque was cut in a Kiki bob. She was wearing a black velvet coat trimmed with what looked like ruffles of maribou fur, and on one shoulder was pinned a bunch of artificial violets. She toyed with a pair of black kid gloves, and squirmed, and looked very cock-sure.

"I think I'll go and gargle, Mamma," the child saccharinely announced.

"That's a dear," said the woman, "but come right back."

"I will," said the child, who minced away, and in passing bestowed a condescending smirk on the Princesse de Villefranche.

"What a horrid little *cochon*," the Princesse mused. As the child disappeared indoors the Princesse noted her stagey walk. She moved in an artless baby way but not like a *bona fide* baby. It was more like the walk of a middle-aged actress in the throes of a dated ingénue rôle at the Théatre de l'Odéon.

The Princesse glanced at the card attached to the adjoining chair to see if she could make out the name of this odious neighboring family. The name on the card, she read, was *Mr. Walter Webster Basch*. He seemed a very odd occupant of a Royal Suite.

No one was occupying the chair at the Princesse's left,

but as she looked toward it a woman approached with a steward who was buried in books and blankets.

"I don't see why you didn't put me on the sunny side in the first place," the woman was complaining to the steward.

"You said you preferred the north side, Madame, because there was not such a wind."

"I said nothing of the kind. There isn't any wind. I should think you would know by now that I always want my chair in the sun. I travel back and forth enough," she added gloomily, sitting down.

"Are you comfortable now, Madame?"

"No," said the woman. "This chair doesn't hit me right in under the knees. That other chair on the north side fitted better."

"Madame, the chairs are all alike."

"They're nothing of the kind. Please bring me the one I had."

"Yes, Madame." The steward soon returned with the other chair. The woman established herself in it and began to read a book. The Princesse noted that the book was *Cosima Wagner* by Moulin-Eckart.

The woman was smartly dressed and looked to be in her middle forties. Her face was arresting and the Princesse thought it resembled Cosima Wagner's. The voice in which she had expressed her dissatisfactions to the steward had been low and carefully modulated and even agreeable in inflection. The Princesse found her speech an absorbing contradiction of form and content. The name on the card attached to her chair was *Mrs. Niobe Why*.

The ship moved on past miles of water, and the Princesse felt like a snooze. With Walter Webster Basch at her right side and Niobe Why at her left, the Princesse Angèle de Villefranche took a nap and had some diverting dreams.

Two days had passed and Napier had not received any word from the Princesse. "She must be a mean old snob," he decided, and dismissed her from his mind. At Victor Zukor's insistence Napier had capitulated to walking briskly around the deck. They walked around and around because there was nothing else to do.

The second morning out Napier had been surprised to find a newspaper under his door. Something world-rocking must have happened, he assumed, to warrant such a phenomenon. He rushed to the door and picked up the paper and anxiously perused the front page. He read there that the Prince of Wales had just laid a cornerstone at Folkstone; that d'Annunzio was suffering from a cold; and that Texas Guinan henceforth was going to part her hair on the right side. For the rest, the paper was largely filled with advertisements of hotels. Later that day a special extra edition was distributed which contained a denial that Texas Guinan was considering a change in her coiffure.

The third day out Napier received a wireless message from Gala Jersey. It read: HUNTING DIVINE ON ANGLOMANIA HOW IS IT ON LETHARGIC BLESS YOU GALA. He went to the wireless office at once and replied: ROTTEN DARLING NAPS.

The fourth day out the Princesse decided to take some snapshots. She had never taken any pictures before and the idea amused her immensely. "Kodak As You Go," she had read in some American magazine, and she had gone straight out to the Avenue de l'Opéra and purchased an Eastman Kodak. She told the clerk that she was always completely bewildered by mechanisms. But he assured her that the Kodak was simple, that all she needed to do was point it at any given object, and push a thing and turn a knob and that was all there was to it. She bought a large supply of films, and Mirabelle mastered the mysterious process of loading and unloading the Kodak.

"Let's try to get Albertine to pose out in my deck chair." The Princesse put on her wrap which was strewn with the diamond-shaped buttons, and set out bearing the cat in her arms, Mirabelle following with the camera.

Albertine was not disposed to "pose," and brushed up against Niobe Why. Instead of complaining, which the Princesse expected, Mrs. Why smiled down at Albertine who immediately leapt to her lap. Several snapshots were negotiated. Then the Princesse pointed the Kodak seaward and took a few views of foam. The result of these activities was that Niobe Why became friendly. The book she had been reading fell to the floor, and the Princesse was surprised to see that it was *Où J'ai Perdu Mon Coeur.*

"It's a stupid book," said Niobe Why, "like all French books of American impressions. The author even writes that the chief articles of American diet are hominy and oysters."

"What *do* the Americans eat?" asked the Princesse cautiously.

"They eat beefsteak and they drink," was the gloomy rejoinder. "Anyway," Mrs. Why went on, "nobody can write anymore."

"Do you do much reading?" the Princesse asked. She never joined in generalities.

"I read all the time. I do nothing but read. Nobody knows how to write."

"Fancy!" said the Princesse de Villefranche.

"Of course I mean by that that no American can write. In France there is still Colette—and Valéry and André Gide. But no one in America knows anything about writing."

The Princesse gave these observations very close attention. She was on the lookout now to glean authentic Impressions. Mrs. Why was a well bred American woman who ought to be a well of authority. The Princesse stored away the fact that no American could write.

It was time for lunch and the Princesse and Mrs. Why went down to the restaurant. They lunched together and arranged to sit at the same table for the rest of the voyage.

Niobe Why was a woman who spent her entire life in outskirts. A divorcee, she divided her time between New York and Paris. In both cities she inhabited the fringe of Society and the fringe of the professional world. Her Social Register friends were perturbed that she knew acrobats and painters. And her friends whom she called the *bums du monde* thought her social connections stuffy.

An expatriate, she considered France the only true Elysium. She groaned every fall at the thought that she must return for a stay in America. Her fortune was in American bonds and she had to go home to collect. Of course she could have arranged to do this in Paris but she chose instinctively the more distasteful process. In the fall she would say, "I have to go to New York for my coupon clipping," employing much the same dejected inflection of her lukewarm sporting friends who said, "We go every year to Norway for the salmon fishing."

Her business matters attended to, she always remained in New York for several months to enjoy "the season." She took her enjoyment in pointing out that each year it grew worse and worse. She would dine with her friends in East Sixtieth Street and complain of the hearty drinking. She would dine with her friends in West Eighth Street and complain that Greenwich Village was gone. She deplored the passing of social barriers as she scurried from lunch with a jazz composer to tea with a straight-laced dowager. She kept up all kinds of "connections," and remained an extremely gloomy woman.

She informed the Princesse that in her opinion there was just one excuse for America's existence. It was the home of the one living mortal she unqualifiedly admired, her friend Aurora Overauhl.

The Princesse was avid and pressed Mrs. Why for

details about her friend.

"You'll have to meet her," said Niobe Why. "Nobody can describe her. She's very extraordinary. She has ideas."

The Princesse gathered only that Aurora Overauhl was *inouie*.

On the fifth day out Napier Knightsbridge received an apologetic note from the Princesse. She had just found his note underneath a pillow, and she was *tout à fait désolée*. Would he come right up and lunch that day with herself and Mrs. Niobe Why?

Napier advised Victor Zukor that he was off to lunch with a Princesse.

"Quit your kidding, old man. I'm from Missouri."

"I thought you said Poughkeepsie was in New York."

"It is," said Victor. "People just say they are from Missouri when they say they've got to be shown."

"Shown what?"

"Whatever it was that made them say they were from Missouri."

Napier went off, allowing that Mr. America was a bit dotty.

Lunch with the Princesse de Villefranche proved to be an amusing experience. She was in her highest spirits, and Niobe Why was less depressed than usual. Another guest at the table was Mr. Wilburton Renegade. Mrs. Why had known the publisher for years, and they had often crossed the Atlantic together. Her returns for her annual coupon clipping frequently coincided with Mr. Renegade's returns to his New York office. He went abroad each year to try "to get some new names for his list." He said at lunch that this year he had got some good new decadent Germans. Next year, he added, he hoped to get a Swiss author if he could find one.

"Biographies and Memoirs will of course remain my long suit," said Mr. Renegade. He was middle-aged, with a mouth that people habitually described as "sensual." And a streak of white through his sleek black hair made him very "attractive to women."

The Princesse did not mention her projected Impressions. She was indissolubly signed up with the firm of Alphonse Oiseau. Perhaps though, she thought, Mr. Renegade might ultimately publish her book in an English translation. She took down his name and New York address and felt she had made a valuable connection.

Talk turned to a misadventure the Princesse had had in signing some papers. A list of questions had been given her to answer as a foreign visitor to America. She had dealt with the matter conscientiously and had filled out the entire blank. To the question, *"Etes-vous anarchiste?"* she had answered, *"Pas du tout."* To the question, *"Etes-vous poly-game?"* she had answered, *"Pas souvent."* Her blank had been returned to her by a solicitous clerk who had read it. He had brought her a fresh blank and had begged her to answer the second question, *"Jamais de ma vie."* She had been reluctant to pen this line but at last had done as she was told.

"You'll have to brush up on evasion," said Wilburton Renegade. "In America it's a necessary evil."

"When you get there, *lie*," said Niobe Why. "Whatever they ask you, lie."

"Why?" asked Napier Knightsbridge.

"It's a code. It's a passkey," said Niobe Why.

"Fancy!" cried Angèle de Villefranche.

Renegade turned a quizzical glance on Napier. "If you're interviewed at the dock," he said derisively, "remember to say the right things. Say you believe in God and the Devil, though everyone will know that you don't. Swear that the Constitution is sacred. No one will expect you to have read it. Say that you're sure that business is sound. Everyone knows that it isn't. And say that there's just one girl in your dreams, and that she's an American Girl. Add that the skyline exceeds your expectations, and everything will be jake."

"What is *jake*?" asked Angèle de Villefranche.

"Broadway for fine and dandy."

"Everything's jake!" cried the Princesse, delighted.

"Oh yeah?" said Niobe Why. She attempted a gangster talkie inflection but it came out chiseled New England.

Wilburton Renegade ordered another round of cherry brandies. "As between polygamy and anarchy," he said, "you'll find it safer to champion anarchy. If you say you're an anarchist people will laugh it off as something nebulous. But if you say you're polygamous that comes down to something solid. It's safer to throw a bomb than to say you're an adept at two-timing."

"What's *two-timing*?" asked the Princesse.

"Harlem for sleeping around."

Niobe Why was distressedly calling a boy to empty an ashtray. "Two-timing is no concern of mine. It's all I can do to get one," she said, looking glumly from Napier Knightsbridge to Wilburton Renegade. The publisher patted her on the hand, and said, "There there. There there."

Lunch over, Napier felt highly exhilarated and warmed by the cherry brandy. The Princesse asked him to dine the next night, and to go with her to the ship concert. Niobe Why declared that ship concerts were the bottommost depths of boredom, but nevertheless the Princesse maintained that she was curious to attend one. Napier agreed to call for her, and descended to his stateroom.

Victor Zukor was naked, as usual, doing something he called the "rope." As Napier came in Victor smelled his breath, and said, thunderstruck, "You're drunk!"

"Not on two glasses of wine and two cherry brandies."

Victor Zukor shook his head and muttered, "Health is wealth."

Napier set out to describe his luncheon, but Victor was not interested. "Feel my *major pectoralis*," he said, but Napier could not be annoyed. "What's the use?" he reflected as he lighted a cigarette. Victor continued his exercise until Napier mentioned the ship concert. The performers, it seemed, were any and sundry passengers who could "do" anything.

"I'd like to be on that bill myself," said Victor very seriously.

"What could you do in a ship concert?"

"I could pose and ripple my muscles."

Napier agreed that this sort of thing might be a relief at a concert.

"Gee, old pal, I wish you could help to get me on that bill." The look in Victor Zukor's eyes was that of a trustful child who wanted terribly some angel food cake.

"Well, I'll see what I can do about it," said Napier, returning to the first-class section. "I might as well do this as nothing at all," he argued with himself.

He consulted a man who sat behind a round brass-grated window, and learned that participants in the forthcoming ship concert were so far discouragingly few. Only three people were scheduled to appear: Madame Armada Menace, the prima donna, Mr. Olaf Andersen, a young Swedish pianist, and Baby Janet Basch, the Sweetheart Kiddy of the Radio Fans.

The man behind the window was very grateful for Victor Zukor. He had not realized that the current Mr. America was on board. Would Mr. Zukor come right up and discuss the matter of his act? A boy was sent down for Victor who came up in a white slipover sweater. He and Napier and the man, whose name was Hodge, repaired to a spacious office which adjoined the florist shop.

"Now, Mr. Zukor, what is it you want to do?" Hodge

began.

"I want to pose and ripple," said Victor Zukor.

"I see you are of statuesque proportions."

"I'll strip," said Victor, pulling off his sweater.

"Oh no, that won't be necessary. I'm sure no one holds the title of Mr. America without good reason."

"Feel my *trapezius*," said Victor.

"Now, about your act," continued Hodge, "I take it you do a species of variety turn in classic poses?"

"I do all the deities in their best-known attitudes."

"I see. Could you make your act last fifteen minutes?"

"I'd just as soon make it an hour."

"No, better fifteen minutes," said Hodge. "Do you require any props?"

"No, but I want a good strong light above my *serratus magnus*."

"Very good," said Hodge, looking a bit uncertain.

"And would you rather have me brown or white?"

"Beg pardon?"

"I said, would you rather have me bronze or marble?"

Hodge seemed hard put to. "Better be bronze," said Napier. "White bodies are going out."

"I wear a tin acanthus leaf and some gold wings on my heels."

"That sounds very fine," said Hodge.

It was then arranged to put Victor Zukor second on the bill, as a filler between Olaf Andersen and Baby Janet Basch.

∽ GOING SOMEWHERE ∽

That night the sea began to roll and the ship set in to pitch.

Madame Armada Menace had dined on a broiler in her suite. Before retiring she decided to take a turn around the deck for exercise. She put on a voluminous chinchilla wrap and a tight chinchilla turban. The deck was sloping now up, now down, but she faced the wind with zest.

As she turned a corner she was face to face with Wilburton Renegade. She had met him once at Aix-les-Bains, and she held out her hand in greeting. To her great surprise the American publisher passed her by and cut her.

Madame Menace surmised the cause of Mr. Renegade's rudeness. Their meeting at Aix-les-Bains had been at Renegade's request. He had invited her to tea in the garden of the Hotel de l'Europe, and had made her a proposition relating to a possible book of memoirs. Madame Menace's life had been picturesque and her account of it would be a seller. The public was always seduced, he said, by a look into the early life of an artist. The process of *becoming* a well-known figure never failed to fascinate the public. Would Madame Menace care to sign a contract?

Madame Menace had brusquely refused. So many *fiascos* had dotted her years that she felt she could not project herself in print in that flattering light which she realized was the essence of autobiography. Mr. Renegade then had made another proposal. Would Madame Menace join him on a boat trip that night and drink some excellent champagne on the near-by lake dear to Lamartine? Madame Menace, she made it clear, would not. Even in midsummer she could not take a chance of catching cold mooning around on lakes.

It was plain that Mr. Renegade was resentful of her refusals to capitulate to his professional or personal offers. In order to avoid meeting him again on deck Madame Menace returned to her suite. She was still worked up over the catastrophe of her recent London recital. The critics had been very cruel and had written that Madame Menace had made an appearance and nothing more. Often before she had been so nervous that she had given outrageous performances. But never before had she left the stage without singing a single note. She thanked her stars that her time was past for facing an audience in the flesh. From now on she was going to have to face nothing but microphones and cameras. She was on her way to New York to appear as the featured prima donna of Abel Hoffensteiner's Canned Opera Company.

The soprano had started out in life as Mary Menace of Liverpool. All her life she had sung, though almost never on the pitch. She was only a child when her parents concluded that she had great "musical talent." But Mary's innate desire to show off was even then counteracted by her fear of being shown off. A sensitive observer might have noted at this time that her soul did not cry out implacably for music. It sought some means of rather explosive personal expression, and music served her ends as well as anything.

(65)

⟲ GOING SOMEWHERE ⟲

As a girl Mary Menace was taken to London to hear *Lucia* at Covent Garden. In the midst of Tetrazzini's ovation which the hectic Mad Scene occasioned, Mrs. Menace made an appeal to her daughter's ego. "Some day, dear, you can do that too. All you've got to do is set your heart and soul upon it."

Mary set them both upon it with an absolute bulldog grip. And in due time she gave a London recital at Wigmore Hall. Her audience filled her with panic, and her performance was disastrous. Jarred, but not discouraged, she consulted a fortune teller. Mrs. Wombat had quarters in Soho and followed her own method of divination.

"Young woman," said Mrs. Wombat, "I can see that you are a five. That means that your fire dominates your water. Now what can I do to help you?"

"Some jinx is at work on my musical career."

"Nonsense! What's your name, young woman?"

"Mary Menace."

"You're doomed to fail unless you change that name. The success of an opera singer lies entirely in her name. The thing to avoid is obvious alliteration. The thing you must have is *concealed* alliteration. Now take Marcella Sembrich. If she had been Martha Sembrich she would be unknown to-day. Her success is based, young woman, on the *cella Sembrich*. Or take Geraldine Farrar. As Fanny Farrar she wouldn't have a chance. It's that *r* perfectly placed in *Geraldine* that acts as her open sesame."

"But what about me?" inquired Mary Menace.

(66)

"You need a first name in three syllables with the *second* starting with *M*. Now let's see: Amelia Menace, Elmira Menace. Ramona Menace. How would that be, I wonder, Ramona Menace?"

"Somehow it sounds Red Indian," objected Mary.

"Then how about Amanda? No—now wait—it's coming—ARMADA!"

"*Armada Menace*—yes, that sounds invincible."

"You can't go wrong, young woman, on concealed alliteration."

Mary Menace was pensive. "There's no alliteration at all in Luisa Tetrazzini. I wonder why it is she has been successful?"

"Young woman, Tetrazzini is a *seven*," snapped Mrs. Wombat. Then she strode to the door and waved good-by to Madame Armada Menace.

The result of this séance was that the singer married Lord Ford, who all his life had been active in British maritime pursuits. He speedily fell in love with this beautiful girl who bore the name *Armada*. His almost immediate death (on a day when Armada was repeating for the forty-fifth time in succession the waltz-song, *Je Veux Vivre*, of Gounod's Juliet), left his widow in possession of his considerable fortune.

Enabled thus to buy her way into impoverished Royal Operas, Armada Menace became a spectacular and highly publicized diva. She specialized in Puccini rôles with which she took extraordinary liberties. In *La Boheme*, a moderately

(67)

short opera, she would have the second act sung twice, appearing, herself, the first time as Mimi, the second time as Musetta, thus indulging herself in her predilection for Musetta's vocal waltz. Critical objection was often taken to her costuming as Minnie in *The Girl of the Golden West,* for she wore an ermine wrap and an Antoine lacquered wig in the famous card game scene in the saloon. Such aberrations served to spread her fame though they failed to win favor for her. And in spite of her wealth and her unique audacity she suffered increasingly from stage fright. She seriously considered pursuing her career under her title, Lady Ford. She felt that the protection of this powerful name might provide her with a greater self-confidence. But in the end her *snobisme* was over-ruled by her superstition. There was no concealed alliteration in the syllables of Lady Ford. And she attributed what renown she had won to the misty wisdom of Mrs. Wombat.

Last summer while resting at Deauville she had met Abel Hoffensteiner. He had broached to her his project for organizing a Canned Opera Company, and had opined that as a drawing card Armada would be just the ticket.

As she lay in her berth in the tossing *Lethargic* Armada Menace hoped New York would be kind.

In the ship concert Armada had consented to regale the passengers with a group of Russian songs. But she demanded to see the program in advance to be sure it contained no typographical errors. The ship printers, she found, had quite outdone themselves, and the program was faultlessly set up:

ᗌ TRANSATLANTIC EPISODES ᗌ

MR. OLAF ANDERSEN

"A DREAM OF ANCIENT GREECE"—Classical Poses

MR. VICTOR ZUKOR
(Mr. America)

BABY JANET BASCH

MADAME ARMADA MENACE

In spite of the storm the passengers were perceptibly
picking up. Travelers were gathering in chattering groups
and discussing their season's projects. Napier Knightsbridge
asked Victor Zukor about his plans for the winter. What
sort of future was opened up by becoming Mr. America?
Victor said he did not know——there was so little precedent.
But what, asked Napier, was the customary fate of the various Misses America and of all the Mesdames Universe?
Victor could not recall what had happened to any of these
Queens. He said he guessed they got married or something.
As for himself, he was going straight to Poughkeepsie for
a week of fêted homecoming. And then he was going to
"tackle New York" and put himself "over big." To begin

with, he knew he could get work as a sculptor's model. He knew one sculptor in New York, he said, who had recently won the *Grand Prix*. (Victor pronounced all French phrases exactly as they were spelled in English, which made for occasional confusion in communication.) He advised Napier to live at a "Y" in New York. He said it would be cheap and clean, and that Napier could play handball and swim. Napier replied that his friend Billy Marvel had engaged a room for him at the Shelton.

"Well, that's okay. You can swim there too," said Victor.

Niobe Why questioned Angèle de Villefranche concerning her New York plans, and she was aghast to learn that the Princesse did not have a plan in the world. The Princesse knew no one in America save the French consul and she had no intention of looking him up. And as for where she was going to live, she thought she would "take a flat."

Mrs. Why decided she would have to take the Princesse under her wing—at least for a day or two to guide her through her first bewilderment. To be in New York and not know a soul Mrs. Why considered "the limit." She advised the Princesse to put up at the Ritz. It would be at least a good springboard. She would be stopping there, herself. And her first night in town Mrs. Why was going to dine at the Wildernesses'. Her friends, Carl and Chloë Wilderness, were giving a small dinner party. If the Princesse would care to go, Mrs. Why could fix it up by wireless. The Princesse consented, and the dinner date was clinched off the coast of Newfoundland.

~ TRANSATLANTIC EPISODES ~

The ship concert was scheduled for nine o'clock, and people were staggering as best they could into the Empire ballroom. The floor of the room was at every angle, almost never horizontal.

The Princesse and Napier and Niobe Why took chairs in the center of the room. Mr. Renegade insisted on standing near the door in case proceedings should become unbearable.

A vast club woman named Mrs. Bushell-Basquette acted as Mistress of Ceremonies. She was returning to New York after a summer of research in Leningrad. She had gone to Russia to drink in local color of the period of Catherine the Great, for she was going to impersonate that monarch at New York's forthcoming Beautiful Arts Ball. And she was bent on doing the thing with no flaws in her authenticity. Bracing herself against a pillar, she introduced the pianist Olaf Andersen, informing the assembled listeners that he was "certain to provide a treat."

The applause as Mr. Andersen finished did not indicate that this prophecy had been correct. No one listened to the Strawinsky sonata save Mrs. Niobe Why, and she said in a despairing voice at the end that Strawinsky had disintegrated. "He has lived too long in Paris," she observed, echoing the echo of an echo.

The pianist had known in advance that his hearers would be bored by the selections he chose. To know he was performing good music well and that his hearers were hating it appealed to his natural *snobisme*. Though at only the outset of his career, Olaf Andersen realized that the piano recital

was a moribund institution. It had started gloriously with
Liszt and was ending honorably with Paderewski. Too
great a mass production of pianists was one reason for its decline. Hundreds of people nowadays played the piano well.
Talented adequacy was the mark of Olaf Andersen's generation. There was little or no supremacy. Facile, even colossal musical technique was abundant. But who of the
younger generation of recitalists could make one ache or
tingle? Proportionately with the increased contemporary ex-
ploitation of music, significant musical accomplishment was
waning. It was of course a tiresome *cliché* to deplore the Last
of the Titans. But at the present time this was more than a
cliché. With the vulgarizing advent of Radio a musical era
was ending. Olaf Andersen realized regretfully that his rôle
was that of a torch-bearer at the end of a procession.

After taking a bow the pianist relinquished the platform
to Victor Zukor. Before the emergence of Mr. America,
Mrs. Bushell-Basquette announced: "We are now about to
be given a view of A Dream of Ancient Greece. In these
Troublous Days of Wear and Tear I Find it is Gratifying to
Note that there Still are Those who Find Time to Uphold
the Greek Ideals. What an Inspiring Experience it is to
encounter a Body Beautiful! We will now welcome Victor
Zukor who Gloriously Carries On the Hellic—or rather
the Hellenic Tradition."

Victor appeared, very lithe and brown, in his wings and
his acanthus leaf, and went through his statuesque poses
with a concentration sublime. He began by reproducing the

pose of the Praxitilean Hermes. He held no child in his arms but the pose was nevertheless recognizable. Then he "flowed" and stood for some seconds as the Apollo Belvedere. He brought his act to a close on the floor in the pose of the Dying Gaul. In response to the wild applause he did some localized muscle rippling. Throughout it all the Princesse was busily wondering why he was called Mr. America. She assumed at last that he must have gained this national name by right of claim in the manner of Anatole France.

Mrs. Bushell-Basquette next introduced Baby Janet Basch. This child was a product of Schenectady and was known from coast to coast. Every Monday night at eight a million radio fans tuned in on their favourite Sweetheart Kiddy. Her weekly broadcasting was sponsored by Gargantua Gargle, Incorporated, and her trip to Europe with her parents had been paid for by her earnings from this Master Mouth Wash.

For her ship concert appearance Baby Basch was wearing a pink dress covered with sequins, which stopped just above her knees. Her manner was one of Olympian self-confidence, and her repertoire featured popular songs of regret and unrequited love.

The Princesse listened absorbedly to the first two songs, but when Janet Basch was midway in the third, the Princesse became confused. "Why is she singing the second song over again?" she inquired.

"She isn't," said Niobe Why. "It's a different song, but

they're all alike."

"Then how can you tell it's a different song?" asked the Princesse.

"You can't," said Niobe Why.

"Then—" The Princesse was anxious to pursue her point when someone behind her went "SHH" so violently that she was silenced and dropped her program.

By now Janet Basch was raising her sugary voice in another number:

"If you left me what would I have left?
   I'd be so blue, be so bereft,
   If your charms were in another's arms
   My arms would be aching to hold your charms. . ."

At this juncture Niobe Why was forced to scurry to the deck. The performance was making her uncontrollably sea-sick.

"There there. There there," said Wilburton Renegade, as he came to her assistance.

Armada Menace, behind a screen, was resenting the easy success of Janet Basch. There she was, the hateful brat, only five years old, and already tasting the joys of public approval which Armada Menace so longed for. The brat had every gift which had been denied Madame Menace. She had poise and assurance and a rhythmic sense, and an ear that made it impossible for her to vary from perfect pitch. She was singing into a microphone even though she was on the Atlantic. The concert was being broadcast so

(74)

that the *Anglomania* could enjoy it.

An exciting experiment was being tried out in the reception of this concert on the *Anglomania*. A professor of applied electricity was on board who was testing his newest invention. It was a small mechanical device permitting the deaf to hear the radio with their teeth. They were to "sip" their music through slender sticks placed in contact with a vibrating mechanism. The device was a vibrator surrounded by rubber and attached to a wire which could be plugged into the sound reproducers. Several deaf *Anglomania* passengers tuned in on Baby Basch successfully, and a message was sent to the *Lethargic* by wireless, saying that a good time was being enjoyed by all.

Pandemonium broke loose as Baby Basch finished. "Isn't she *cute?*" fat ladies panted as they beamingly beat their palms.

At the end of her group the child obliged with an encore, choosing a ballad of optimism designed to make everybody happy. She cavorted in front of the microphone and simpered through the popular hit, *Singin' with the Wolf at the Door*.

"Singin' with a pain in the neck," said Wilburton Renegade who was feeling a bit bilious himself. Mrs. Why had recovered, and had now returned with the publisher to the ballroom entrance. Consulting her program, she saw that Madame Armada Menace was next, and that her first number was the aria, *Aller Au Bois Cueillir La Framboise*.

"Hasn't she had the raspberry enough without hunting

(75)

it in the woods?" Niobe Why gave vent, as was her occasional wont, to a somewhat somber wit.

Armada Menace climbed onto the platform slowly. It was pointing alarmingly uphill. She wore a gown of silver cloth with two trains, one on either side. Her eyelids were painted a delicate mauve, and the lobes of her ears were rouged. She wore a heavy barbaric gold necklace, and carried a fan on which was painted a scene from the troubled romance of Heloise and Abelard.

She began the aria and Wilburton Renegade nudged Mrs. Niobe Why. *"Singin' with a Frog in the Throat,"* he said, "should be the name of this number."

Near the end of her group Madame Menace forgot all about the microphone. She moved back and forth on the platform striving only to maintain her balance. She reached the climax of her final song in a veritable roar of sound:

> "I call aloud thy name
> That all the night may hear . . ."

With a far-flung gesture she crashed the microphone violently to the floor. And as she backed away, bowing, she entangled her feet in her wealth of trains and fell. A gasp went up from the audience, but the singer was not hurt. She rose and took a few more bows, and conceded that it might have been worse.

Early the following morning Armada Menace was out on deck. She had had a sleepless night which no sedative could remedy. Throughout the night her resentment of Janet Basch had nightmarishly mounted. At dawn she had felt she could strangle the brat with no slightest qualms of conscience.

The sea had calmed down and most of the *Lethargic's* passengers were still asleep. Madame Menace paced tumultuously the B deck which was deserted.

Janet Basch came out by herself and seemed to be looking for something. She smirked at Madame Menace and said she was searching for her silver flask. She always kept it full of Gargantua Gargle, and she had lost it somewhere on the deck.

Armada Menace felt her wrath on the upgrade. She looked out to sea and exclaimed, "I see a whale!"

"Oh where?" said the child. Her head did not quite reach the top of the wooden railing.

"Out there—don't you see it?" said Madame Menace, as she lifted the child and perched her on the railing's edge.

"I don't see a thing," whimpered Baby Basch.

Armada Menace made the most of her sudden opportunity. She gave a slight push and Baby Basch fell into the sea with a splash. Armada brushed her hands as though to wipe away a stain. Then she turned and looked behind her to make sure no one had seen.

Smoking a pipe, ten feet away, stood Wilburton Renegade. Armada Menace, horrified, had immediate visions of prison. The publisher could be counted upon to persecute her to the limit.

(77)

✃ GOING SOMEWHERE ✃

Mr. Renegade approached and gallantly threw his pipe into the Atlantic. "Good morning, Madame Menace," he said. "I would like to shake your hand."

As the two clasped hands the *Lethargic* heaved in sight of Sandy Hook.

NEW YORK

SEASON

I

NEW YORK CITY ROSE OUT OF the sea looking like nothing on earth. The Princesse decided this was the only adequate way to describe it.

A few reporters came on board to put questions to Madame Menace. And two journals had sent photographers who requested the diva to pose. Armada knew she was not looking her best, but she felt that she ought to be gracious. To her interviewers she said that she was looking forward eagerly to her début in the new Canned Opera. She hoped to make her initial appearance in one of her Puccini rôles. Puccini, she said, was to her mind the greatest composer who ever lived. Last summer she had made a pilgrimage to his grave at Massacuccioli, which without any doubt was the most unusual grave in the world. It was concealed behind an upright piano in the living room of his villa, and everything in the room was just exactly as he had left it. On a table reposed the composer's glasses and a fading copy of *Vogue*. And his Scotch terrier named "Max" kept waiting endlessly at the door. Armada said there was no place sadder except Liszt's house at Weimar.

The only other passenger on board who rated interviewing was Mr. Wilburton Renegade who sometimes was good copy. He was not particularly articulate this year, and made some standardized statements. The public was reading better books all the time, and striding ahead, he said.

The Princesse, after her first sight of skyscrapers, took them quite for granted. Before disembarking she ran to the back of the boat and photographed Hoboken. Her baggage was casually opened and quickly okayed by the customs officers. But she had to wait on the dock an hour for Mrs. Niobe Why. All of this lady's luggage was opened and exhaustively examined. She was forced to pay some duty and this made her feel very low. The Princesse did not mind waiting because so many things intrigued her. The most absorbing thing of all was a sign reading: WALK YOUR HORSES. What in the world could it mean? This occupied her for most of the hour.

At last all luggage was cleared away and the passengers disappeared. Napier Knightsbridge was met by Billy Marvel and Yvonne Débris. Victor Zukor slapped him goodby and added, "See you soon." He promised to ring him up at the Shelton as soon as he returned from Poughkeepsie.

Armada Menace made for the Ambassador, feeling de-

cidedly wrought up. The drowning of Baby Basch had
been hushed up and pronounced an accident. It would
have been very bad publicity for the *Lethargic* that Sweetheart Kiddies could fall off her.

The Princesse de Villefranche and Niobe Why drove
off in a Luxor Cab, with Mirabelle and Albertine and the
baggage following to the Ritz in a Paramount Cab. Mrs.
Why rang up her friend Chloë Wilderness at once to let
her know that she and the Princesse had arrived. Mrs.
Wilderness said, "How nice!" and added that dinner would
be at seven. It had to be early because she was taking her
party on to the theater.

Carl and Chloë Wilderness were possessors of a few
million dollars, and they lived in East Fifty-second Street
in a house just off Park Avenue. Mr. Wilderness spent his
days in Wall Street and his wife gave innumerable dinners.
Excellent dinners they always were, with fine wines and
impeccable service.

The Princesse and Niobe Why were punctual and arrived at the house at seven. Mrs. Wilderness herself did
not appear until a quarter of eight. In the interim the
Princesse studied the first American home of her acquaintance. The house was done over completely to resemble an
Italian Renaissance *palazzo*. Mrs. Why sat down on a
carved wood chair and said she was most uncomfortable.

The only other dinner guests were the two Van Dongen
twins. They were twenty-five years old, and heirs to one
of the most staggering Fifth Avenue fortunes. They arrived

at a quarter past seven, and their entrance made the Princesse gasp. She had never in all her life seen two such ravishingly beautiful people.

The sister, Anna Van Dongen, came in closely followed by her brother Annesley. They were both very blonde, and their handsome faces looked like reproductions of each other.

Cocktails were served, and Carl Wilderness said that his wife would be down any minute. At the end of half an hour the lady appeared, encased in innumerable yards of flowered chiffon. She walked with a flowing grace and had a fragile beautiful face. Her eyes were blue and hinted that they had looked for years at the crescent moon.

She greeted the Princesse graciously and embraced her friend Mrs. Why. "Niobe, dear, how *are* you?" she said with a bright-eyed smile.

"A year older than when you saw me last, Chloë."

"I think I've never seen you looking better," said Carl Wilderness.

"I always show a healthy flush when I've a tinge of fever."

Another round of cocktails consumed, the party went in to dinner. Midway in the meal talk turned to the question of whether Ethel Barrymore were "great."

"I think she is very great," said Chloë Wilderness.

"Well, Chloë," said her husband, "the word *great* is a great big word. If you use it on Ethel Barrymore, what will you have left for Duse?"

"Duse's dead. She died in Pittsburgh," observed the Princesse.

Disregarding these affirmations, the hostess changed the form of her previous utterance. "If Ethel Barrymore is not great then I do not know who is."

Niobe Why announced that in her opinion no living actress was great. The great days of the theater were over.

Anna and Annesley Van Dongen simultaneously put the same question. When was it, they asked Mrs. Why, that the theater had gone under such a cloud?

"Well, I should say that it ended with Rachel."

"How can you have seen Rachel if she died before you were born?" inquired the Princesse.

Mrs. Why looked up at the maid and said she would try a pickled pear. She then changed the subject abruptly and said, "Chloë, how is Aurora Overauhl?"

"I scarcely know how to answer," Mrs. Wilderness looked puzzled. "We haven't seen her for weeks. She has moved to the most outlandish address over on the East River. And it seems she is not going out at all and she's seeing almost no one. I'm told that at times she just sits silently and thinks for quite a while."

"A real eccentric," Carl Wilderness said concisely.

"But I can't understand it," Mrs. Why seemed quite stunned. "I must look Aurora up as soon as I'm settled."

After coffee and liqueurs the hostess told her guests that they were going to a Gilbert Miller production. She did not specify what the play was. For her the word Miller was an equivalent of Sterling or Cartier.

A distressing accident had befallen the Wildernesses' chauffeur that afternoon. He had been run over while standing in parley with a Park Avenue traffic cop. He had not been seriously injured, but still he was unable to function that night. Carl Wilderness said that he, himself, would drive his car to the theater. Anna and Annesley Van Dongen had their own sport roadster outside. They started to the play, and the rest of the party was to follow shortly.

Driving to the theater proved to be an extremely involved affair. They had to go east before they went west, for Fifty-second was a one-way street. And once they had reached the West Fifties Carl Wilderness recalled that the Gilbert Miller production was in Henry Miller's Theater, and this was in West Forty-third Street, which was exclusively west-bound. Thus in order to enter this thoroughfare they had to return to its source at Fifth Avenue. This accomplished by slowly crawling through congested honking traffic, they found they were not allowed to park in the vicinity of the theater. So they drove for a mile until they found a spot where parking was permitted. They descended here and hailed a cab and returned in it to the theater. These operations had taken up more than an hour, and they missed the first two acts of the Miller Production. The Princesse could not figure out what it was about, and she never learned the title.

After the play Mr. Wilderness offered to drive the two ladies to the Ritz. But inasmuch as his car was a mile away,

Mrs. Why begged him not to bother. Good-nights were said on the sidewalk in front of a cafeteria. In the window dead fish were arranged in a pattern which spelled the word SUPREME.

Encaged in a cab, the Princesse said she was feeling very lively. She could not bear the thought of returning to the Ritz, and she wanted to go to Harlem.

"There's not any sense in going to Harlem," objected Niobe Why. "Harlem is now all over with. Everyone up there is white."

But the Princesse was childishly insistent, and finally Niobe gave in. She asked the driver where to go and he suggested the Cotton Club. The ladies looked very well dressed, and he thought this club was about their speed.

Half way through the Park the Princesse saw a card on the wall of the cab. It read: PUSH THIS BUTTON IF YOU WANT ENTERTAINMENT. The Princesse immediately pressed the button and the cab became filled with entertainment. A jazz-band in Philadelphia was fiercely broadcasting *Why Did You Have to Go?*

Arriving at the Cotton Club, the ladies were about to enter, when the doorman stopped them formally and asked if they had no escorts. Two ladies alone, he said, could not be allowed in the Cotton Club.

The Princesse de Villefranche immediately misunderstood his meaning. "May one go in alone?" she asked, through purely selfish motives.

"No, ma'am," said the doorman.

"May three go in together then?" the Princesse anxiously inquired.

"No ma'am, lady, no women alone goes into the Cotton Club."

"Can one man take two ladies in?" the Princesse still pursued him.

"Yes, ma'am."

The Princesse gave a sweeping look up and down Lenox Avenue. She stopped a rotund colored man who was singing to himself.

"That's no use, lady," the doorman said. "*He* can't go in with you. No colored people is ever allowed inside the Cotton Club."

"I thought it was a colored club. Our taxi driver said so."

"Yes ma'am, it's a colored club, all right, but no colored folks is allowed."

"Fancy!" said the Princesse de Villefranche.

"Just *what*," said Mrs. Niobe Why, "are the qualifications for entrance?"

"Your party, ma'am, must be sexually mixed, but racially uncompounded."

Mrs. Why looked whipped and said, "Well there, Angèle, I ask you."

Just then a taxi pulled up at the curb and its driver was obviously Latin. "We'll ask *him* to escort us," the Princesse said, as she waited for the occupants to descend. When at last they climbed out of the cab they continued a conversation with the driver. The man was Wilburton Renegade, and his partner was a cutie. Mr. Renegade was asking the chauffeur whether he was aware of the significance of his name. His license card informed the world that his name was Tomasso Gatto. The chauffeur said he knew that it meant tom cat, and that he was extremely proud of it.

"With my best wishes," Mr. Renegade said, as he tipped him a five dollar bill.

"I say, don't let him drive away," cried out Angèle de Villefranche. "We can't get in without a man, and that one looks delightful."

"There there," said Wilburton Renegade. "You come along in with me." He introduced his girl friend who was known as Delight Wheeleright.

The floor-show of the Cotton Club was at its noisiest height. The band was emitting blood-thirsty shrieks that made the Princesse dizzy. The colored girls were dressed fantastically as feathered Navajo Indians, and were throwing their arms, and shaking their hips, and singing away for dear life. A short time later they came out again attired as Spanish gypsies.

"When do they appear as Negroes?" inquired the Princesse.

Miss Delight Wheeleright faced her squarely and answered, "Don't be silly."

The Spanish gypsies disappeared, and something quite different followed. A colored boy with light brown skin did a traditional Chinese sword dance. In contrast to the other dances, there was nothing incongruous about this one.

(87)

The boy was a skilful performer and commanded immediate respect. He was beautifully made, he had dignity and poise, and his face was clearly chiseled and slightly wistful. The Princesse was moved, and she felt that this boy had a quality of unbearable poignance. She recalled the first time she had seen Nijinsky in Paris twenty years ago. This brought to her mind the lovely Eve Lavallière who had recently died. The thought of this actress brought her back to the talk about actresses at the Wildernesses' dinner.

"Who is this Ethel Barrymore?" she suddenly inquired.

At this Miss Delight Wheeleright gave the Princesse up. "Can't we ditch the nut?" she whispered to Wilburton Renegade.

When the show was over Mr. Renegade suggested going somewhere else.

"Can't we go some place low?" the Princesse begged.

"There's always some place where people are going, but it's always a different place," said Mr. Renegade.

He added that there was one block in Harlem which was filled with low-down cabarets. There were four of them all in a row, and they alternated in popularity. One month one place would be popular and the others would be deserted. Then in some unfathomable manner people would switch and favor another. The places were known as The Bloodstain, The Inkwell, The Black Hole, and The Glimpse of Hell.

"Where are people going this month?" he asked a taxi driver.

"To The Black Hole, mister," replied this sensitive creature. A driver less perfectly attuned to the life and times of his customers might have answered, "Nassau," "Morocco," or "Palm Beach." This driver knew his New Yorkers however, and he never made stupid mistakes.

Mr. Renegade and Miss Wheeleright and Mrs. Why and the Princesse jolted off to look in at The Black Hole.

Napier Knightsbridge was pleased with his room at the Shelton and opined that the view was superb. After dining with Billy Marvel and watching a performance of *Get Up and Rest* (the show was still selling out and prospering) he waited for Billy in the wings, and they then visited a speakeasy around the corner from the theater. They walked down three steps and knocked four times and said they were friends of Julia. They were promptly admitted and sat in a kitchen where they drank two or three gin fizzes. As they left Napier was given a small blue card which would serve to admit him later. He went back to this place the following week, but the building had been torn down.

"Now, let's go to Harlem," said Napier.

Billy Marvel hailed a cab and gave the driver an order. "Go to The Black Hole," he said.

The Black Hole was a basement in Harlem which resembled innumerable others. But at present it had been singled out as a fashionable *rendez-vous*. It comprised two

rooms, both very small, and an almost inaccessible washroom. The basement was entered through an elaborate arrangement of bolted doors, provided with slots to be looked
through. People had to be looked at before being admitted,
but everyone was always let in. The front room contained
an upright piano and half a dozen tables. The back room
contained the same number of tables and a small but well
stocked bar.

In its atmosphere the place suggested none of the horrors of its namesake in Calcutta. It was moderately clean,
and its tables were covered with blue and white checker-
board cloths. Above the bar hung photographs of Snake-
hips Tucker, Cora La Redd, Paul Meeres, Baby Cox, and
other celebrated people.

Boasting only twelve tables, The Black Hole was designed to accommodate forty-eight customers. But a hundred people were always there and all of them always got
tables.

The entertainer at The Black Hole this season was a
girl named Narcissus Cook. She was big and black with
a comic-strip face, and she sang and played the piano. She
was blessed with unusual vitality and she worked it day
and night. She sang at The Black Hole every night from
midnight until seven the next morning. Then she snatched
a brief sleep, and her forenoons were often taken up by
recording for phonographs. In the afternoon she would frequently officiate at distinguished white cocktail parties,
and in the evening she often appeared in vaudeville turns

in Harlem theaters. She wrote her own song material and
projected it in a manner all her own. It was usually a varia-
tion upon an elemental theme.

As Napier and Billy Marvel were admitted into The
Black Hole, Narcissus Cook was in the midst of one of
her best-liked numbers:

> "I'm gonna get a bran' new Aeroplane Papa
> To make my propeller go roun',
> I said—to make my propeller go roun'."

The air of the place was heavy with smoke, but people
could be distinguished. There were well-groomed white
women in jewels and fur wraps, and lumbering black truck-
drivers. At one table a famous Broadway operetta star was
surrounded by variegated admirers. Most of the crowd were
Harlem habitués, but a few were nervous first-timers.

Through the smoke Napier Knightsbridge and the
Princesse de Villefranche discerned each other simultaneously. She was at a corner table with her group of friends,
and Napier and Billy approached. Miss Wheeleright was
introduced to Napier, and Billy was introduced all around.
Nobody "got" his name. He and Napier were assigned an
adjoining table, and sat down with their backs to the wall.

Across the room, facing them, sat the young pianist Olaf
Andersen. Beside him glared a strange looking woman with
surprisingly bright green hair.

Confronted by so many familiar faces, Napier Knightsbridge was moved to exclaim, "This place looks just like

the first-class bar after dinner on the *Lethargic*."

"It looks to me like the Algonquin at lunch," said Miss Wheeleright, scanning the crowd.

Niobe Why said it looked to her like Park Avenue at tea time.

"It looks like nothing I've ever seen," said the Princesse de Villefranche.

"It looks like hell," said the green-haired woman accompanying Olaf Andersen. "It looks like hell, and hell looks like hell, and hell how I hate Harlem."

"Who is that woman?" the Princesse asked. "I think she is delightful."

Wilburton Renegade said she was a well known sculptress whose name was Lenore Lanslide.

"Well known is good," said Delight Wheeleright.

"How extraordinary," said Napier. "I've got a letter of introduction to her."

"Well then you'd better mail it to her," said Wilburton Renegade. "The little lady's in no mood to-night for making social contacts."

Napier returned his gaze to the woman and studied her now in detail. The most striking thing about her appearance was her closely cut grass-green hair. At a party at the house of a painter one time Mrs. Lanslide had capriciously squeezed a tube of green oil paint into her hair. She had been highly pleased by the color effect, but the stuff was annoyingly sticky. She was obliged at last to shave her head to remove the oil paint from her hair. When the hair grew out sufficiently later, she had it dyed the same shade of green. It was perfectly straight and cut in a bang across her forehead in the manner of Foujita.

Mrs. Lanslide's eyes were steely gray, and their lids were made up bright blue. For the rest her face was alabaster white, with full lips painted orange. In its chromatics her face approximated a Barnum and Bailey poster.

As earrings she was wearing two small gold fish which were embellished with human breasts. She had forty silver bracelets on her right forearm, and seventeen on her left. Her evening gown was made of jade beads, with a practically nonexistent bodice.

Mrs. Lanslide finished her fifth gin fizz, and said in a throaty voice, "I swear to God to-night's the last night I'm ever coming to Harlem. If there's one thing this side of hell I hate it's a crowd of dirty niggers. Say do I hate it— sitting around every night up here with a crowd of black and white bums. Listen here—I'm going to find something else to do—I'm going to look up some Mongols."

"Don't talk so loud, Lenore," said Olaf Andersen.

"Say who are you—say what the—say—what do you think you're—listen—now don't try to tell me what to do—I'll give you the woos woos woos."

Olaf Andersen looked embarrassed and ordered another drink. Mrs. Lanslide went on in a voice which seemed doubly arresting and emphatic, because in speaking she never permitted herself the slightest gesture. The words poured out in a stormy stream but her body remained quite rigid.

"I want to find some Mongols to mingle with—I wonder who knows any Mongols. Do you know any Mongol music?" she turned to Olaf Andersen.

"No, I don't," he said.

"Well why the hell—well why—why don't you know any Mongol music? I suppose you think that because you play Strawinsky that's enough. Well listen dearie, I got beyond Strawinsky ten years ago. Arnold Schoenberg and the lousy Six are just old shoes to me. I'm sick of all that truck—I want to hear some Mongol music."

"Isn't she amazing? Did you ever hear anything like it?" asked Billy Marvel.

Mrs. Lanslide was continuing. "I've got to the place where I can't bear to hear a thing but Mongol music. I don't know why the hell you've never learned any Mongol music. It's so vicious and monotonous—I'll bet you've never heard any. Say cutie, see here, tell Mamma why it is you don't know any Mongol music."

"Oh be quiet," said Olaf Andersen.

"You be quiet yourself—say listen—who's giving this party—you or me?"

"I'm sick of this place. Let's get out," said Olaf Andersen.

"Not on your life you don't get out. God, how I hate Harlem."

A woman wearing glasses at a near-by table quietly turned to her escort. "I don't see why people come to places like this if they have color prejudice."

Lenore Lanslide overheard these words and threw a biscuit at the woman. "You shut your face, you dowdy frump. What do *you* know about Harlem? You look to me as if you'd never before been out of Flatbush. Now listen here—don't talk to me about Harlem and color prejudice. I came to Harlem before it was built—I even discovered Harlem. How many Negroes have *you* ever known—answer me—I *ask* you—how many? Well I've had every Negro in Harlem for dinner and plenty for over the weekend. If I hate Harlem it's not because I've got any color prejudice. I hate it because I'm woos woos woos and I want to meet some Mongols."

"What a terrifying person," the woman said. "I think we'd better be leaving."

"Oh, let's wait a little longer. Something may happen," replied her escort.

A youth from the operetta star's table wandered over to Mrs. Lanslide. He was well known as a clever juvenile in pretentious musical comedies. "You seem to be having a swell time, Lenore," said Colbert Tulle.

"Don't come around getting fresh with me—you'll get it in the woos woos woos."

"But my dear girl—"

"Don't my dear girl *me.*"

"Well then, my terrible looking wreck, I hope you get dee tees. I hope you'll drink like a fish until you have to have your ankles tapped."

"That's the stuff—sit down here, cutie," said Lenore

Lanslide making room for Colbert Tulle. "I've just been reading a book about Mongols. Do you know any Mongol actors? I'm so woos woos doing the things I do I want to do something else."

"Well, I'll write you a song," said Colbert Tulle, and he started in to sing: "What wouldja do if you didn't do what you do do? And who wouldja do if the last one hadn't been a hoodoo? What wouldja do and who wouldja do and who'd do hoodoo doodle doodle doo. . . ." His voice drifted off, losing track of the rhythm.

"Oh Tulle—you ought to be shot."

"I am—half shot."

Narcissus Cook was pounding away and growling another of her songs:

> "I'm gonna get a bran' new Submarine Papa,
> To counteract my undertow,
> I said—to counteract my undertow."

A plump white woman sitting near the piano knew the words of all Miss Cook's songs. She joined very lustily in the frequent refrains which began with the words "I said." At the end of the song she got up and crossed the room to Wilburton Renegade. "Are you Wilburton Renegade?" she asked. "Somebody just pointed you out."

"Yes, I am."

"Well I just wanted to tell you how much I always enjoy the books you publish. I simply loved that life you put out of that sizzling skirt, Nell Gwynne."

Mr. Renegade gave his admirer a very snooty look. "I suppose you're the reading public," he said. "Have you ever read *Mother Goose*?"

"No, but I've read *Mother India*," the woman promptly replied.

Lenore Lanslide cried out across the room. "Say dearie, that was a swift one." She faced Mr. Renegade: "Have you ever read the book called *How to Grow Up Though Handicapped*?"

"That to you," said Wilburton Renegade, flinging her a chicken bone. He had known Mrs. Lanslide for several years but they were not on the best of terms. He had knocked her down at so many parties that finally she had got sore. The bone he threw her was carried away by Toad, The Black Hole's cat.

"Come here, Toad," said the proprietor, William Mt. Sinai, better known as Barnacle Bill.

"Toad is a toadess," observed Lenore Lanslide, in a tone that sounded oracular.

"My name is Imogene," the fat woman told Mr. Renegade. "Please call me up any morning." She wrote her telephone number on the back of a soiled menu card. "I'm usually in by seven o'clock in the morning." Then she swayed away from his table, and focused Lenore Lanslide. "Your hair is certainly the pajamas," she informed that lady with a smile.

"You're pretty hot yourself, Mrs. Egg," said the sculptress.

"My name is Imogene Pulley. What's yours? Just a minute, I'll give you my number. I'm almost always at home in the morning, but I haven't been this week. I don't know why it is I just can't manage to get home this week. I hope my kids will know enough to go out to the delicatessen. Have you got any kids? I've got two little kids. They're cute little bastards, both of them. I call them Ruby Lavonne and Olive Geneva. Gee, I hope they're safe and sound. Wait a minute, I'll give you my number."

"I'll give you the air if you don't clear out," threatened Lenore Lanslide.

"Do you mean to say you don't want my number? Then you've got a mitigated mentality."

"Say what the—who do you think you are? Say listen—what do *you* know? What do you know about anything? Who are you to talk? I'll bet you don't even know who's king of England."

"Sure I do," replied Mrs. Pulley, "I know damn well. It's Paul Robeson." She returned to her table, her shoulders shaking in uncontrollable mirth.

The door was unbolted by Barnacle Bill, and Gala Jersey came in. She had with her a sheik from a colored cabaret whose floor show had just ended. All his good points of physique were emphasized in an outfit resembling a rainbow. He wore a striped red and green silk shirt, and a bright blue tie on which was painted a naked white lady in the act of climbing a tree. His revealing suit was of light gray worsted, and he wore five diamond rings. His skin was the color of Hershey almond bars, his expression a trifle sulky.

"Darling. Angel," whined Gala Jersey, seeing Napier through the haze.

"Gala! How divine!" said Napier, blowing her a tender kiss.

"I want you and Billy to meet Racy Bumpus," she introduced the sheik. "He's known as God's Gift to Fifty Million Frenchmen."

"Don't you simply *love* it up here?" asked Billy Marvel.

"Gala darling," said Napier, "that woman over there is the sculptress Lenore Lanslide."

"How absolutely divine," said Gala Jersey.

Napier introduced Gala and her acquisition to his friends at the adjoining table. "She's someone else," he told Mr. Renegade, "who has a letter to Lenore Lanslide."

"I don't know why you go on like this," said Wilburton Renegade. "Nobody comes to New York any more with letters of introduction. You just hang around in Harlem and in time you meet everybody. Not a very long time either," he added.

Gala Jersey approached Lenore Lanslide and said, "I've a letter to you from Olympia Lunt."

"Well isn't that cute?" said Lenore Lanslide. "And what is that one up to?"

"She said she thought you might be interested in a life of Benvenuto Cellini."

"Well isn't she bright! Have a chair. Have a drink. Good old Benvenuto Cellini. Say what a life that old bird led."

"Wotta life!" chimed in Imogene Pulley.

"Oh you. Shut up. Who are you to talk."

"Well I guess I've read his Memoirs. I read them aloud to Agnes Whitcomb. I guess I know my Cellini."

Mrs. Lanslide had a sudden inspiration. "Cellini meeny miny mo, catch a nigger by his toe—that means you, cutie," she kicked a neighboring colored gentleman. "If he hollers—say why don't you holler?—let him go. Eeny— I mean Cellini meeny miny woos woos woos." She picked up Toad and sat her down on the table in a pool of spilled gin fizzes.

"I want to go home," said Olaf Andersen. "I've got to do things to-morrow."

"Got to go home and practice, I suppose. Don't you ever get through practicing? Why the hell do you practice all the time? You'd think you were five years old. Why don't you grow up and snap out of it, cutie, and learn how to woos woos woos."

At this moment three South American big game hunters were admitted into The Black Hole. They were all in drag but their entrance caused no more than a flurry of interest. They were wearing showy dresses covered with rhinestones, and all three waved immense feather fans. They were on their way home from a ball where a thousand other gentle- men had been similarly bedecked.

∽ NEW YORK SEASON ∽

"I think this place is God-forgotten," said Mrs. Niobe Why.

As if in answer, two policemen crashed in, and The Black Hole was speedily raided. A hundred people were there, but fifty managed to get away. The rest were crowded into a patrol wagon and driven away to a night court.

The names of the fifty criminals were demanded, and all of them gave false names. "I'm Madame Curie," said Angèle de Villefranche on the advice of Wilburton Renegade. Lenore Lanslide informed the judge that she was Madame Butterfly, while Colbert Tulle made it most emphatic that he was Sothern and Marlowe. The judge was aware that this must be false, but was not in the least disturbed.

"Five dollars apiece as a fine for disturbing the peace in a nuisance," he ordered. Each of the fifty prisoners produced a five dollar bill. The judge counted the money carefully to be sure it was correct. Then he split the pile of bills in two and put half of them in his pocket. The other half he handed over silently to Barnacle Bill. This transaction over, Barnacle Bill led his customers back to The Black Hole. Raids like this one were frequent occurrences, bearing certain resemblances to fire drills.

The Black Hole had been padlocked for an hour, but now it was open again. In the interim Narcissus Cook had worked out a new ditty. She was nearly raising the roof with her shouts as the customers trooped in again:

⌒ GOING SOMEWHERE ⌒

"I'm gonna get a bran' new Elevated Papa,
  An' ride in the open air,
  I said—an' ride in the open air!"

Things progressed very much as before. People were considerably drunker now. This was the only difference.

Lenore Lanslide stood up and asked a waiter, "Where's the Astor?"

"At Broadway and Forty-fifth Street, Madame."

"Oh I don't mean that Astor—I mean the ASTOR—I mean the you know—I mean the woos woos woos."

The waiter then directed her to the washroom.

Two years ago Lenore Lanslide had made a theater date with one of her models. They agreed to meet in the lobby of the theater which was in West Forty-fifth Street. Lenore Lanslide had been on time, but her young man was a little late. She pitched into him with vengeance and asked him why he was late. He replied, embarrassed, that he had gone across to the Astor to wash his hands. From that time on Mrs. Lanslide always referred to washrooms as Astors. She could not believe that by now there was anyone in New York who did not know of this practice.

By the time she returned from the Astor, The Black Hole was looking pretty disheveled. Imogene Pulley was smashing her plate with the wooden handle of a fork; the big game hunters were dancing together, all three embracing each other; Gala Jersey and Racy Bumpus were lying entwined on a bench; Colbert Tulle was playfully running around mopping up spilled gin; Olaf Andersen had fallen asleep

(*102*)

with his elbows on the table; the operetta star was flat on
the floor, her gown strewn with French-fried potatoes and
soaking in Scotch and ginger ale. Someone had knocked the
table over on her, and she had not bothered to get up.

"Well, young man, this is Harlem," said Wilburton
Renegade to Napier. "Ten years ago all this would not have
been possible."

"Ten years ago was the time to come up here," Mrs. Why
announced to the Princesse. "Aurora Overauhl started coming to Harlem and then the whole city followed. Of course
she never comes near it now. Her investigation of Harlem
has caused its present disintegration."

"Fancy!" said the Princesse bewilderedly.

"This sort of thing in Harlem is bringing people closer
together," threw in Imogene Pulley who was now engaged
in putting the fragments of her plate together again.

"Closer together is good," said Delight Wheeleright, as
she cast an envious glance at Gala Jersey in the sheik's em-
brace.

There was a ring at the door and Barnacle Bill admitted
another party. Olaf Andersen awoke, and was surprised to
see the pianist Mr. Amherst Archduke. He was a very distinguished and well established pianist with an international
following. He had played that night in Carnegie Hall, and
was now uptown to enjoy the rewards of accomplishment.
He was accompanied by an oft-divorced lady named
Amethyst Dudley-Frankau-Tingle. She was swathed in
ermine, and vainly sought to avoid stepping in the fried

potatoes. At that moment Olaf Andersen felt that he would never make the effort to play in Carnegie Hall. He was already tasting the joys with which such efforts seemed to be crowned. The paths of glory led, in the end, to the same basement dumps in Harlem.

"What about the Cellini?" Gala Jersey faced Lenore Lanslide.

"Swell," replied the sculptress.

"When may I look in?"

"To-morrow, cutie. I'm giving a cocktail party. You come too," she turned to Racy Bumpus. "Hold on, what did you say your name was?"

"Gala Jersey."

"Oh I see—so *you're* the Jersey Lily. And what's your name, Blackberry?"

"He's Racy Bumpus," said Gala.

"God's Gift to *you*, Mrs. Lanslide," smiled the sheik.

"May I bring all these people at these two other tables?" asked Gala, indicating Napier and Billy and the Princesse and Mrs. Why and Mr. Renegade and Miss Wheeleright.

"Sure—bring the whole woos woos woos."

The entire party then broke up and went through the ordeal by checkroom. Imogene Pulley drew in a deep breath and seemed about to utter something weighty. She quivered from head to foot and at last she exploded. "Baby!" she said.

On the sidewalk Olaf Andersen raised his hand to summon a cab.

"Say what do you think you're doing—why the semaphoring? Are you trying to pull a Kreutzberg? Listen, cutie, what do you think you're up to?"

"I'm hailing a cab," said Olaf Andersen faintly.

"Do you think I'm going home at four o'clock?" cried Lenore Lanslide. "Say what do you think I am—a vestal virgin? Get a move on your little woos woos woos. We're going to The Glimpse of Hell."

II

The next morning Mrs. Philistine Johnstone-Casey was reading her New York Times. She was still in bed, but the sun streaming in gave witness that the day was well advanced.

Mrs. Philistine Johnstone-Casey's bed took the form of a golden swan. The foot of the bed was the head of the swan, and the head of the bed was its tail. The sheets were of sheer pink *crêpe de chine,* the pillows of frail pink lace.

Turning to the page of Society news, the lady made an interesting discovery. The *Lethargic* had just arrived in port, bearing Madame Armada Menace. Mrs. Johnstone-Casey said significantly to herself, "I must go on my errand to-day."

On the opposite page of the paper she was attracted to a small but arresting advertisement. It was introducing a toilet preparation which made sun tan last all winter.

"Ah well, that's not my problem," observed the lady.

∽ GOING SOMEWHERE ∽

Philistine Johnstone-Casey was utterly black.

The recent rapid growth of Harlem and its mushroom manner of development had caused a formidable increase in real estate values. By judicious buying and selling of property over a period of twenty years, Mrs. Johnstone-Casey had amassed an enormous fortune. She wielded a powerful influence in Harlem, and was even a power in Wall Street. Her appearance greatly enhanced her position, for her bearing was superbly regal. With pronounced but pure Ethiopian features and a somewhat heroic body, she looked every inch an African Empress, born to subjugate unruly jungles.

The telephone rang at the side of her bed. Wilburton Renegade was on the wire. "Good morning Mr. Renegade . . . Fine, thank you. . . . You were loud and wrong last night? . . . Yes, Mr. Renegade . . . That would be splendid . . . Some night next week . . . Yes indeed, ah'll be delighted to meet her . . . You bring her up one night next week . . . Will you be at Mrs. Lanslide's this afternoon? . . . Well, that's fine, ah'll see you there . . . Not at all, Mr. Renegade . . . Good-by."

Utopia Lux, Mrs. Johnstone-Casey's ward, appeared to inquire who had called.

"That bastard Wilburton Renegade. He wants to bring up another princess."

"That makes the fourth this fall," said Utopia Lux.

Utopia Lux was the color of coffee after two teaspoonfuls of cream. Her build was of the kind described as "bouncing." She was mountainously fat, with ripples and billows of wildly oscillating chocolate flesh. Her face was round, with miniature features, and slightly resembled a kewpie's.

Miss Lux had begun her musical studies at Oberlin, Ohio. From there she progressed to Boston where she attended the New England Conservatory of Music. Her voice was a high soprano of a pure and appealing quality. She learned various oratorio rôles, and sang them with colored choirs for several seasons in the South. One night at a *soirée* at The Dark Tower in Harlem she sang *He Shall Feed His Flock*. The song was transposed very high in order to fit into the singer's register. Mrs. Johnstone-Casey, always on the lookout for talented members of her race, thought this girl showed remarkable gifts, and promptly took her under her wing. For two years Miss Lux had studied in New York at Mrs. Johnstone-Casey's expense. An afternoon song recital in Town Hall had been the culmination of these efforts. The critics all wrote that Utopia Lux was a very commendable musician.

Mrs. Johnstone-Casey had set her heart on introducing Utopia into the Metropolitan Opera Company. She was about to make an appointment with its directors when she read of Abel Hoffensteiner's project. Perhaps his Canned Opera would be a more readily accessible goal for Utopia.

She showed Miss Lux the Times announcing Armada Menace's arrival. Then she telephoned Abel Hoffensteiner and made an appointment for that afternoon.

At three o'clock her mauve Rolls-Royce drove up for Philistine Johnstone-Casey. "Go to the Gotham Colosseum building in West Thirty-fourth Street, Samson." Her chauffeur bowed low, and the lady was soon rolling down Seventh Avenue.

Abel Hoffensteiner sat in his office, perplexed by the appointment he had made. He figured it out that the rich black woman probably wanted to book a box for his season. He decided he would have to refuse her request, and was getting himself primed to be firm.

Mr. Hoffensteiner had recently arrived in New York after many successful years in California. He had been a producer of "presentations" at a movie palace in Santa Barbara, and his name had become a world-wide symbol for ultra-lavish prologues. With the coming of talkies he had slightly varied his habitual tactics. Instead of putting operatic music to presentation purposes, he put on an opera itself. As a prologue to Garbo's *Anna Christie* he staged *The Flying Dutchman* which seemed to him appropriately marine. It was sung in a condensed version but it had an immense success. So the second week he ordered his singers to perform the opera without cuts. *Anna Christie* was then eliminated because the bill was too long.

Eventually Mr. Hoffensteiner decided to organize a permanent company and invade operatic New York. He had gone as far as he could staging operas as a concomitant of movies. He would now inaugurate a season of movies in the form of grand operas. He came on to New York and took a careful stock of the situation. It seemed to him that

Canned Opera was just the thing that the public wanted.
The American people were making it clear that they liked
things removed from reality. They showered their favors
on shadows of actors, but neglected these performers in the
flesh. They sat by the millions listening to radios and records, but recital audiences were diminishing. So he did not
see how his venture could fail in contemporary New York.

As a home for his company Abel Hoffensteiner took over
the Gotham Colosseum making no effort to redecorate it.
Opera houses, in his opinion, should be conventionally ornate and musty. He planned to run his season in the manner
of the Metropolitan. There would be an extensive repertoire,
with different works each night, repeated in rotation
throughout the winter. And the shooting of the operas was
to take place in a sound studio in Astoria.

Mr. Hoffensteiner did not need to borrow funds to
finance his undertaking. By extraordinary luck in the stock
market he had recently quadrupled his fortune. The stock
of Universal Can had gone up by leaps and bounds. Abel
Hoffensteiner owned one third of the shares. Who had the
actual control was obscure.

At a quarter of four arrived at his door Mrs. Philistine
Johnstone-Casey. She was wearing a commanding black
velvet cape and a glittering silver turban.

"Ah suppose you know who ah am," she addressed the
impresario. She said "ah" instead of "I" for calculated reasons. She realized that among her white acquaintances she
passed as something exotic. She felt she might as well, in

one word at least, sound typical of her race. She realized too that a slight accent always helped to ingratiate a member of one people into the favor of another. "Witness the case of Nazimova," she would often say to herself.

"Certainly, Mrs. Johnstone-Casey. And what can I do for you?" He indicated a chair and they both sat down.

"You can engage Utopia Lux for your coming season."

Abel Hoffensteiner sat silent, stupefied.

"Ah suppose you have heard of Miss Lux? She's a very superior soprano."

Mr. Hoffensteiner said he had seen her name in various musical periodicals. He added that his list however was complete, that there was no room for any more artists. Besides, a colored soprano would hardly fit in anyway.

Mrs. Johnstone-Casey argued that these reasons were fallacious. There was always room at the top, she asseverated. And the days of color prejudice were rapidly passing. She reminded him that there were distinguished and widely appreciated colored poets, novelists, actors, blues and spiritual singers, dancers, architects, pugilists, lawyers, and superlative Negro dentists. But at present there was not a single colored operatic diva. Mr. Hoffensteiner should appreciate his opportunity.

"Unthinkable," said the impresario. He then gave Mrs. Johnstone-Casey a learned dissertation on the subject of how singers nowadays entered the great opera companies. They either came in, he said, by the weight of an already world-famous name, or else their entrance was paid for by influential financial backers.

"That's just what ah mean, Mr. Hoffensteiner. Ah'm an influential financial backer. Ah'm out to advance mah ward's career and ah'll back her to the bitter end."

The impresario said it was quite impossible.

Philistine Johnstone-Casey faced him squarely. "Ah suppose you know ah control Universal Can?"

Abel Hoffensteiner blanched.

"If you don't engage Utopia Lux *ah'll liquidate!*"

The impresario felt faint and wiped his brow.

"Engage Miss Lux or ah'll tell what ah know about your bullish maneuvers. You sign her up or ah'll raise such a stink!"

Mr. Hoffensteiner drew up a contract. Perhaps if Miss Lux could sing the title rôle of *Aïda* things would not be so bad.

"What rôles is your ward equipped to sing?" he inquired.

Utopia Lux, it seemed, had so far mastered only two rôles: The Queen of Night in *The Magic Flute,* and Violetta in *La Traviata.*

"A black Queen of Night! A black Violetta! Oh God," cried the impresario.

"Mah ward is not black, Mr. Hoffensteiner. She's a very superior brown. You remember there was once a famous colored singer whose name was Sissieretta Jones? She sang at the old Academy of Music and was known as The Black Patti. Now ah want you to bill mah ward Utopia Lux as

The Brown Bori."

"Oh God," moaned the impresario.

"She must sing on the opening night, of course."

"It's in Madame Menace's contract that *she* sings on the opening night."

Mrs. Johnstone-Casey slightly tapped her foot. "Miss Lux will appear on the opening night or ah'll liquidate instantaneously."

"All right, I'll arrange to have them both appear on the opening night."

"Ah call that right genteel, Mr. Hoffensteiner." She affixed her name to the contract as a proxy for her ward. "Now, when shall Miss Lux come down for her audition?"

"Her *audition*? Miss Lux has been engaged."

"Nevertheless ah want mah ward to come down and have an audition. She's all coached up on *Addio del passato*. Ah don't want it said that Miss Lux succeeded on account of any favoritism."

It was then arranged that Utopia Lux should come in the following day. Mrs. Johnstone-Casey swept into her car, and said to herself, "Ah've done it!" She ordered Samson to drive her across town to Lenore Lanslide's cocktail party.

III

Lenore Lanslide (née Poucher) was a product of Chicago, the last of a line of highly prosperous meat-packers.

∾ NEW YORK SEASON ∾

From her lineage and from her native city she had inherited a quick intelligence, a shrewd business sense, a terrific vitality, a taste for strong language, a thirst for blood, and a heart as big as a house.

Having manifested as a child a rather surprising taste for "art," at seventeen she was sent abroad to be finished. In Paris Lenore enrolled at the Beaux Arts, the Grande Chaumière, and the Colarossi Academy simultaneously. She was over there to get all there was to be had. At that time the most respected master was Rodin, and Lenore turned out one sculptural work more or less in his manner. It was called *The Foot of God,* and it depicted a colossal foot of deity about to descend on a squirming mass of humanity. Most of the mortals betrayed terror or fear. A few were philosophical and were shown engaging in amorous adventures.

Some time later Lenore had come under the influence of Brancusi. She sought "purity of line" and polished away on some birds for several months. Then she modeled a perfect cylinder and a still more perfect cube. She entitled these works *Woman* and *Man,* and sold them for a flattering figure.

It was shortly after this that she artistically found herself. She had dabbled enough in contemporary influence. Symbolism, cubism, significant form, and other artistic *cachets* of this kidney were not for her, she concluded. She was a realist, an accurate representationalist. One day in the Luxembourg Gardens she pounced upon a sailor, took

(113)

him straight home, and turned out a most literal likeness. She called this creation *The Unknown Sailor* and she knew she was now in her *assiette*.

At the Deux Magots she made the acquaintance of Robespierre Lanslide. This French-American gentleman was a literary agent who worked at trying to market the writings of Americans living in Europe to the numerous American publishers who were traveling in Europe. He and Lenore were married one June for reasons forever occult.

On the death of her parents who were shot by gangsters, Lenore returned to America. She squared away family affairs in Chicago, and settled with her husband in New York. They purchased a four floor house in the Murray Hill section, near Madison Avenue. Adjoining the house was an elegant old stable which Lenore remodeled as a studio.

Her social career in New York was started among her husband's acquaintances who were literary people of every denomination. They came in alarming numbers to Lenore's first New York party, and the hostess had an extremely dreary evening. All the authors present spent their time throughout the party trying to seduce the book-reviewers in one way or another; the book-reviewers concentrated on the editors of periodicals, begging for particular books they desired to review for personal reasons; the publishers all went after authors who were on other publishers' lists, and sought to lure them into breaking their contracts. No one paid any attention to Lenore, so she got quite drunk by herself. She had never been actually drunk before, but this literary party started her off.

Prohibition taking effect at about this time was a spur to everyone's drinking. Lenore Lanslide drank more and more—more than anyone she knew. She could outdrink all her friends because of her almost inhuman vitality. Her vitality had swiftly worn her husband down to a fragile wreck. He occupied the top floor of the house and was practically never seen. He and Lenore now met once a week, on Sunday nights at supper.

Lenore had rapidly advanced as a sculptress, and she was now at work on what promised to be the masterpiece of her career. A band of enterprising business men who had dealings with Argentina had decided to present that nation with a token of commercial good will. An heroic sculptural group, they considered, would be an appropriate tribute. They described their project to Lenore Lanslide and were satisfied with the plans she submitted with designs for the projected monument.

Lenore conceived presenting Argentina with a group of forty-eight figures. These figures would stand for the forty-eight states and each would be slightly symbolic. Illinois, for example, would be holding some corn; Alabama would be handling some cotton. The arrangement of all these figures for a time put a problem to the sculptress. She finally decided to allow the figures to follow the geographical layout. California would stand at the extreme left, and so on across the continent.

It seemed only logical to Lenore that the size of each state should also be considered. As a model for Texas, the largest state, she would have to procure a giant. Rhode Island would obviously have to be a dwarf. The others could mostly be normal. By now she had lined up forty-seven models who came up to the necessary requirements. She still had to find a superlative model to pose as the state of New York. She was also obliged to look for a midget to serve as the more or less extraneous District of Columbia.

In order to make the entire group loom visible at once, she was posing the figures on a flight of steps, like a finale of the Folies-Bergère. She had set to work some months ago on this most ambitious conception. At first she worked on one state at a time, but she found she lost sight of the whole. She now was working with all of the forty-seven models posing at once. Wherever she went she kept looking for models for New York and the District of Columbia.

Over her ten-year career in New York Mrs. Lanslide had become quite a landmark. Her behavior was always spectacular and her appearance alone was startling. She had, of course, her critics who condemned her for leading "an irregular life." As a matter of fact she led a life of the strictest regularity. In spite of habitual late hours at night she was always up in the morning. She sculptured each day until four o'clock and then she would dress and go out to cocktails, or else have a party at home. Her evenings and nights were invariably given over to Bacchus.

People would shake their heads and say that she could not go on like this. But she *had* gone on like this for years, and seemed none the worse for wear. If her eyes looked a little more hollow each year she would simply increase their makeup. She was well aware that interesting ravages were more attractive than blanks.

Gala Jersey and Racy Bumpus were due at the Shelton at five. They were stopping to pick up Napier Knightsbridge to take him on to Mrs. Lanslide's party. They did not show up until six because Racy had to take time for breakfast.

They arrived at Lenore Lanslide's at a time when things were getting well under way. Some guests were taking a staggering departure. Others were hopefully barging in. The newcomers caught no sight of their hostess, and they stood for some minutes neglected.

One end of the room was filled with possibly thirty or forty guests. The din that was coming forth was something thunderous. There were so many people and they had to stand so close together and they had so many things to say because none of them had seen each other since yesterday that they were all obliged to raise their voices and shout.

Most of the guests were well-known people, and some were first-rate celebrities. The novelist Catulle Danger was there with his wife, Alla Moscow. Their friends in New

York were always referred to rather sweepingly as "the Danger set." There was also a Cuban caricaturist who signed his drawings "Pup." There were smart looking actresses such as Dot Scott and Viadella Fenestra. Each of them went up to Catulle Danger and told him she was writing a book. A Spanish poetess named Conchita Aragon was looking extremely severe. The Ethiopian, Philistine Johnstone-Casey, was surrounded by a Caucasian court. There were brokers and dancers and aviators and divorcees and music critics and heiresses and hangers-on.

More newcomers kept streaming in, shouting greetings to their friends. "Hello, how are you?" asked Clyde Cavalier of Estelle Limb.

"How are *you*?" answered Miss Limb.

"Hello Estelle, how are you? I'm glad to see you," said Anatole Waterman.

"I'm glad to see *you*. How are you?" said Estelle Limb.

"Fine. How are you?" said Salammbo West.

"Oh hello Sallie, how are you?"

"I'm glad to see you," said Mrs. West.

"How have you been?" said Leslie West.

"How are *you*?" answered Willow Plume.

Amethyst Dudley-Frankau-Tingle came in wearing very long false eyelashes. These black embellishments looked very exotic against her golden hair. She made her way self-consciously through the crowd around the bar. "Hello, how are you?" she said to right and left.

"Fine, thanks, how have you been?" people answered

without looking up.

Several people came up to Napier Knightsbridge and said, "Hello, how are you?" They were all complete strangers but Napier said, "Fine, thanks." He heard no one saying anything else.

A group of six young Negroes arrived carrying various oblong black cases.

"Park your packages in the hall," said Lenore Lanslide, emerging from the Astor in a green oilcloth cocktail jacket. "Hello, there, Jersey Lily," she cried, "come and meet some charming people." She summoned the caricaturist. "Come here, Pup, and meet these charming children. This is Mr. London Bridge, and this is the Jersey Lily, and the black-berry at the right is just God's Gift. There you are. This is Pup," she said in closing.

"When shall we begin, Mrs. Lanslide?" inquired one of the young Negroes.

"Start right in this minute, cutie. The drinks are all on the table."

Angèle de Villefranche and Niobe Why arrived with Wilburton Renegade. They pawed their way through the crowd in the direction of Philistine Johnstone-Casey.

"Ah'm pleased to meet you, Princesse," was the black lady's greeting. But she was frankly disappointed that the Princesse wore no crown. The dictates of that mysterious restraining force which went by the name of "taste" had forced Mrs. Johnstone-Casey into repressing her own long-ings towards ostentation. Instead of the green feathers and flaming satins in which she would have loved to stride across the vision of a dazzled city, she dressed herself in relatively sober garments designed by a disciple of Chanel. It was only rarely now that she broke loose and fastened a bunch of scarlet poppies on her hip. What remained of flamboyance in her nature she had turned into the channels of her vocabulary. She never used a short word if a long one would suffice. And her sentences, when she felt she was on display, were resplendent with sumptuous verbiage. "Mr. Renegade must bring you uptown some night, Princesse, and we'll investigate a limb-loosener."

"A *limb-loosener?*" the Princesse looked startled.

"That's just a term we have for shindig, Princesse—one of our Ethiopian idiosyncrasies. Ah'd take you uptown tonight, but ah've got a previous engagement posterior to this tea."

A bald-headed man approached Napier Knightsbridge and said, "Are you Dorian Gray?"

"Yes," said Napier, too confused at the moment to think of anything less feeble. He turned away and was faced by two extremely chic young women whom Lenore Lanslide had the presence to introduce. They were great pals, these two, she said,—Tulip Wuthering and Fay Rumbelseat. They were Jewish young women and were usually affectionately referred to as Leopold and Loeb.

But a song interfered with pursuit of conversation. Salammbo West was starting in to croon. She and her husband were a unique couple in the Danger set because

they had a child. Salammbo was now bent on showing
Grosvenor Plume how she put her child to sleep:

> "Bow-wow goes the doggie,
> The doggie goes bow-wow,
> The doggie goes bow-wow,
> Bow-wow goes the doggie,
> The doggie goes bow-wow."

Grosvenor Plume deserted Mrs. West at this point, fear-
ing that he might follow the precedent of her child. But
Mrs. West did not mind, and went on singing to Leopold
and Loeb.

"Awoos woos woos," Lenore Lanslide summed things
up, giving her party an approving glance. She then was
called to the telephone. Roddie Oddbody was on the wire.
This architect wanted to know if it would be all right if he
brought along a newsboy. The newsboy was pretty, he said,
and was writing a book.

"Why sure," said Lenore. She had scarcely hung up
when the telephone rang again. It was Gwendolynne
Herscheizer. She wanted to know if it would be all right
if she brought along her laundryman. He was such an
enchanting Chink, she said, and he had the most piercing
eyes. Also, he was writing a book.

"Bring him along," Lenore urged her. "I'm dying to
meet some Mongols." Mrs. Lanslide was always pleased
to see new faces at her parties. The more mixed-up the
party was the better she considered it. This attitude derived

from the failure of that first fatal literary party. Since that night she had never given a party for one exclusive set of people. She considered the world a cocktail and she liked to mix it and shake it. Sometimes the resulting mixtures were not too satisfactory, but at any rate they were better than just straight gin.

Returning to the party she saw that she must chide Salammbo West. That lady was raising a God-forsaken racket:

> "Ee-aw goes the dong-key,
> The dong-key goes ee-aw,
> The dong-key goes ee-aw,
> Ee-aw goes the dong-key,
> The dong-key goes ee-aw."

Mrs. West was now addressing a wider audience, and she showed every intention of exhausting the barnyard in inexhaustible stanzas.

"Shut up or clear out or pipe down and forget it or else woos woos woos," suggested her hostess.

Angèle de Villefranche looked around from time to time and murmured, "Fancy!" She could hardly contain her wealth of new Impressions. "I'm taking them in almost faster than they can come," she said to herself.

Viadella Fenestra and the caricaturist, Pup, were discussing the æsthetics of humor. Their discussion was growing so heated that they were both becoming quite bitter. Simultaneously another group was having a chat about sadness. It had started with Iris Cavalier's description of a singer she had heard at some party. A singer whose name was Clarissa Goode had sat down in a hard-boiled gathering and, accompanying herself, had sung with surprising effect a song about daisies. The lyric, Mrs. Cavalier added, would have looked like drivel on paper. It was all about loved ones at rest under daisies and the Lesson of Life and all that. But Clarissa Goode had so moved her hearers that the party had broken up in tears. "It was just too out-of-this-world," Mrs. Cavalier concluded.

Grosvenor Plume declared that no woman's singing could ever move him to tears. But he confessed in a tipsy manner that he sometimes wept over Rupert Brooke.

Olaf Andersen divulged that he very seldom read any verse. The saddest thing he could recall in prose was Timothy shooting his Uncle Leander's woodcock in *The Grandmothers*.

Tulip Wuthering opined that li'l Edna Mouth was the saddest character in fiction. Saint Laura de Nazianzi, she added, was the second saddest.

"The Marquis de Sade was the first sadist," observed the Princesse, tuning in belatedly on this conversation.

Disregarding the Princesse's contribution, Niobe Why announced that everything on earth was so sad, she didn't see why they were taking the trouble to specify.

Wilburton Renegade asserted that the saddest sight in the world was his glass. It was empty except for an olive. This relatively lengthy and sequential exchange of ideas was now interrupted by a slapping scene.

Roddie Oddbody had arrived very tight with the news-boy, and said he had been insulted twenty-eight times. To this Mrs. Lanslide countered with, "Oh please!"

"I've been insulted twenty-*nine* times!" cried Roddie Oddbody.

"I'll make it thirty," screamed Salammbo West, giving him a slap in the face.

Roddie Oddbody was so heartily incensed that he slapped her promptly back. At this her husband Leslie West came up and slapped Roddie Oddbody. "Take that," he said. "Take *that*!" said Roddie Oddbody, slapping Leslie West. Then Salammbo slapped Roddie again, and he slapped her back again, and then her husband slapped Roddie again until they were all tired out.

"You deserved to be slapped," said Leslie West to Salammbo, "but I couldn't just stand by and allow him to slap my wife. All the same, I'm glad he did." This delicate distribution of gallantry explained, they all three progressed amicably to the bar.

"When shall we begin, Mrs. Lanslide?" asked a Negro.

It was nearly seven o'clock and Mrs. Lanslide now was not entirely herself. "Now listen here," she said, "can't you think of anything else to inquire? All you do is woos woos woos and keep asking me when you begin. Begin right now. Go on and begin. Run along over to the bar and begin."

"You want us over there by the bar?"

"I don't want you anywhere. Who the hell are you anyway?"

"You don't seem to be aware, Mrs. Lanslide, that we're the band from The Glimpse of Hell."

"Well who the hell cares? Go back and give it a good long glimpse, and vamoose and awoos woos woos."

"But you engaged us to play at this party."

"When?"

"Last night."

"Wasn't near The Glimpse of Hell," said Lenore.

"Yes, we were, Lenore," said Olaf Andersen.

"Well well," marveled Mrs. Lanslide, "so I engaged a band!"

"You paid us in advance," the Negro reminded her.

"Say, what a Rothschild I was last night. All right—go ahead and begin."

The men took their instruments out of their cases and began a piping hot scat-song version of *Singin' with the Wolf at the Door.*

Gwendolynne Herscheizer started in to dance with her laundryman, Gin Sin Fun. "I'm going to cut in on that Mongol," said Lenore Lanslide.

Viadella Fenestra roamed around the room inviting everyone present to her cocktail party the following afternoon. People then began to clear out. But Estelle Limb was blocking the exit, engaged in conceiving a dance. She was by profession an interpretive dancer who interpreted Protestant hymns. She argued in defense of her choice that all other music had been interpreted. To *Count Your Blessings* she was now working out a provocative panto-mimic routine.

Mrs. Johnstone-Casey was making elaborate prepara-tions to depart. "Thank you so much, Mrs. Lanslide," she said. "It's been a real impeccable little affair."

"It's been divine," whined Gala Jersey. "And what about the Cellini?"

"Swell," said Mrs. Lanslide.

"When shall I bring it?"

"Awoos woos woos," said Mrs. Lanslide.

A commotion had started near the piano. The newsboy wanted to go away with Leslie West. Salammbo West and Clyde Cavalier had gone to the Astor to compare their appendicitis scars. They returned to find Leslie West fight-ing off the newsboy.

"Don't hurt that boy," said Salammbo West. "If he wants to go with us we'll take him."

"Not to-night, baby," said her husband. "I'm not in the mood."

"Let me look at him. Isn't he horrid! Of course we'll take him. I like him. I want him like a rabbit. I'll tie him up."

"No you don't want him," said Viadella Fenestra. "Just look at him. He's a little beggar."

"Sure he is. I want him. He's a horrid little beggar. Never seen such a swell little beggar."

"Don't you want that boy to accompany you all?" asked

Philistine Johnstone-Casey.

"God, no," said Leslie West.

"Then ah'll wind up your predicament, Mr. West. You just leave it to me—ah'll *lean*." The massive black lady pinned the boy to the wall and leaned against him with all her might. He howled as Leslie and Salammbo West went out. By now Mrs. West had formulated another chaotic desire. "Let's go to the morgue and pass out," she suggested, "and have people come and identify us."

At this juncture Fay Rumbelseat fell downstairs and rolled right on outdoors.

In the street Napier Knightsbridge spoke to Catulle Danger: "I had no idea it was going to be so rough."

"*Rough*, young man?" answered Catulle Danger. "You ought to go to one of her parties sometime *at night*."

Niobe Why was in distress because she had lost the Princesse. Angèle de Villefranche had wandered off by herself around the block to take a look at the back of the Morgan Library.

Her last guests departed, Lenore Lanslide did not calm down at once. She started the phonograph and put on Bessie Smith's *I Want Ev'ry Bit of It*. Watching her reflection in a copper-backed mirror, she started in to dance. Alone, up and down the room, she danced grotesquely over empty glasses.

When exhausted, she looked around the room to see what her guests had wrecked. About a dozen glasses were broken and olive seeds lay in the upholstery. The white satin-covered coal-boxes in front of the fireplace were covered with lost caviar. And a row of fragile blown glass prizefighters was splintered on a window sill. In the Astor she found the havoc a little more serious. Somebody had broken the music-box contraption which was ingeniously attached to the plumbing. When it worked it played *I'm Forever Chasing Rainbows* each time the chain was pulled. The perfume bottles on a dressing table were in bewildering confusion. Clyde Cavalier and Salammbo West had mixed all the scents to see if they could achieve an aphrodisiac. The result of their experimentation now was spilled on the green tile floor. A number of framed old costume prints were splintered in the bathtub. Roddie Oddbody had thrown them at the tub to see whether or not they would bounce.

Having estimated the financial loss occasioned by these damages, Lenore Lanslide now examined her rooms for objects left as recompense. She found that Tulip Wuthering had left forty dollars worth of a new Molyneux perfume which really was far more desirable than the ingredients spilled in the bathroom. Dot Scott had lost an expensive lighter in the crevice of an arm chair. Grosvenor Plume had dropped his billfold containing a hundred and ten dollars. And Amethyst Dudley-Frankau-Tingle had left behind two tickets for the Vanities. These pasteboards were worth ten dollars apiece, and were good for that night's performance. Lenore rang up Gin Sin Fun at once and told him to meet her at the theater. "And don't hang around in the Astor either," she advised the bewildered Chink. She then cleared the broken glass out of the tub and prepared to take a bath. On the whole, though her party had not been particularly eventful, she reflected with some satisfaction that at least it showed a consoling profit.

IV

The following day the Princesse de Villefranche suffered a disappointment. The snapshots she had taken on board the *Lethargic* turned out to be utter failures. When she brought them home from the pharmacy where she had had them developed they proved to be dozens of shadowy likenesses of vague little diamond-shaped objects. The Princesse was desolated, and it took her some time to figure the matter out. In the end it was plain that the clerk who sold her the Kodak had not been explicit. He had told her to point the Kodak at the object, but had not said which way she was to hold it. She had held it backwards, she was forced at length to conclude. The Princesse had crossed the Atlantic Ocean photographing her buttons.

The cocktails at Lenore Lanslide's party had made the Princesse feel squeamish, and she determined to drink no gin to-day at Viadella Fenestra's party. She sent Mirabelle to Mrs. Why's bootlegger to buy a bottle of absinthe. Absinthe was the only liquor which she liked and which did not upset her.

At five o'clock, with her bottle of absinthe tucked in under her arm, she hailed a cab and started off to Viadella Fenestra's. At Fifth Avenue the cab was halted because a monster parade was progressing up that thoroughfare. The driver advised the Princesse that the delay was apt to be lengthy. So she paid him off and climbed out to the sidewalk to watch the parade go past.

Up and down the Avenue, as far as she could see, the sidewalks were jammed with lookers-on whom policemen controlled with clubs. And whirlwinds of torn up telephone directories were blowing from every window. In the street itself innumerable organizations were parading *en masse*. The Princesse tried but was not permitted to walk across the Avenue. "I say, is it almost over?" she asked a neighboring shop-clerk.

"How do you get that way?" replied the shop-clerk. "It's only started."

When the sun had set under West Forty-Fifth Street the procession reached its climax. In an open car beside the Commissioner of Police sat Miss Winona Outing. The Wisconsin Wonder was smiling her thanks for her marvelous homecoming parade. She had won the title she set out to capture, and was employing her famous breast-stroke in blowing kisses to right and left.

A corpulent man came up to the Princesse and complained to her very bitterly. He said he was manager of a Fifth Avenue shop and that parades were ruining the business. No traffic was allowed on the Avenue, he said, and nobody came inside shops. What was worse, the clerks themselves spent all their time on the sidewalks. A few weeks later this shop went bankrupt because a golf-player came home.

"Fancy!" said Angèle de Villefranche, consulting her jeweled wrist-watch. She saw that the time was seven-thirty. And this, she considered, would be too late to go to a cocktail party. Alas, the naïve French Princesse did not know how wrong she was.

The crowd was breaking up roughly now, and scattering in all directions. A burly boy bumped into the Princesse and dislodged her bottle of absinthe. It smashed on the curb and the contents flowed in green rivulets into the gutter. She walked away as fast as she could and bought an evening paper. Then she hurried into a restaurant to escape the smiles of the crowd.

She sat down at a glass-topped table and picked up the menu card. On it she read:

NOT WITHOUT COOKS

"We may live without poetry, music, and art; we may live without conscience and live without heart;

"We may live without friends; we may live without books; but civilized man cannot live without cooks."

Thus sings Owen Meredith in his beautiful poem, *Lucille,* and singing, strikes a responsive chord in the hearts of those who dine at CHILDS.

"May I buy this menu?" the Princesse asked the hostess. "I want to quote it in my book of Impressions." The hostess thanked the Princesse for her interest. If she would leave her name they would send her the menu every week. For every week it bore a new quotation.

"Imagine!" exclaimed the Princesse, and she tipped the hostess two dollars. She ordered some corned beef hash, and turned her attention to the evening paper. The front page was featuring news about Gandhi and rebellious Hindu activities. The Princesse passed these columns by. World news did not interest her. A small-type headline near the bottom of the page piqued her curiosity: "POPE PIUS WELCOMES AMERICAN SAILORS." The Princesse read this item:

> Vatican City—(A.P.)—Pope Pius XI always receives sailors with pleasure because the successor of St. Peter himself can be regarded as a fisherman. So the Holy Father yesterday told a representation from the American Naval Squadron anchored in the Bay of Naples who came to see him.
>
> He recommended to the sailors an Italian book by Father Antonio Stoppani entitled *The Purity of the Sea and Atmosphere*. He concluded with the remark that he greeted the sailors with real pleasure because they were the hope of their country.

The Princesse was delighted by this somewhat bizarre revelation. She opened the paper and perused an inside page. A headline in thick black letters seized her attention:

∾NEW YORK SEASON∾

"BEDROOM LOVE BUNK BUXOM PEACHES' PLAINT—CHECKS SHOW PROOF OF PEACHES' PUDDING." What this could mean she had no idea. Across the page another headline struck her: "FAT FEAR JUMP OF BEAUTY PROVES FATAL." And in the adjoining column: "FELT QUEER SO HE PUSHED MAN OFF 'L' PLATFORM."

"Fancy!" said the Princesse, turning another page of the paper. "GRILL DEFENDANT ON FIVE NEW WOMEN," she read. And "KNOCKING THE NORTH YAM-CONSCIOUS JOB OF BLONDE FROM GEORGIA." "THREE CRY NO TO BEDROOM AL-LEGATIONS." "AIMEE TO SPAR WITH THE DEVIL TONIGHT."

"*C'est inouï, tout ça,*" the Princesse murmured, stopping to see what was on the Women's Feature Page. One column was designed to be read by Mothers. To-day's article was "KEEPING THE NORMAL BOY NORMAL." The Princesse skipped this feature. A department headed "Domestic Hints" suggested "PUT THE TWANG OF FRESH RHUBARB INTO YOUR BROWN BETTY TONIGHT." "*Ah non, c'est trop fort,*" said the Princesse. A fourth column informed her: "A PING PONG ERA IS UPON US." And a paragraph encased in a box inquired: "HAVE YOU EVER HAD AN INTERESTING EXPERI-ENCE? FIVE DOLLARS APIECE WILL BE PAID FOR WINNING LETTERS."

On another page in the largest type that she had seen so far, the Princesse read the warning: "DO NOT BARGAIN WITH YOUR SLEEP." She did not read on to see that this was an advertisement for expensive beds. Next, on the theater page, she read: "FRANCES ALDA SINGS AND OLD MEN WEEP."

She did not follow this up far enough to learn that Madame Alda had been gracious enough to sing at a Bowery Mission. She stopped for a casual glance at the sporting page: "KING OF 175-POUND BOYS TO BE PICKED IN BUFFALO BATTLE." And the line which puzzled her most of all was: "ENERGY VICTOR, DINNER DANCE NEXT—ALCHEMIST OUTRUNS FRENCH LASS." How was she to know that this referred to winning horses in an out-of-season derby? She folded the paper in high bewilderment and was surprised to see her food. It had been on the table for twenty minutes, and now was depressingly cold. She folded up the menu inside her news-paper, and returned in a haze to the Ritz.

That evening she spent in jotting down various notes for her Impressions. The past two days had been so full, she was fairly overflowing. In a little black notebook which she purchased especially for this purpose, she put down scat-tered facts which later she would enlarge upon.

The Princesse noted down for her forthcoming book that "Walk Your Horses" was American slang for *"E Vietato Fumare."* And that it was customary for American guests to arrive at dinner before their hostess; that American dinner table talk was largely devoted to actresses; that practically everyone in Harlem was white; that all the best people were arrested in Harlem every night, but that no one knew it because they gave false names; that Chinese laundrymen rather than Argentine tango dancers were favored by Ameri-can women as gigolos; that rich black women were on hand at parties to *lean* if the occasion demanded; that courses in

Literature were conducted gratis by Fifth Avenue restaurants; and that all American newspapers were written in an obscure code.

After a week at the Ritz the Princesse removed to Tudor City. The lighted signs: TUDOR CITY—FRENCH PLAN had immediately captured her fancy. She sub-leased for the winter a furnished penthouse which was topped by Tudor cupolas.

On snowy nights she would stand on her terrace and look out on the world's greatest scene of unreality. Straight down, on one side, lay the black East River bordered with millions of bulbs. In the other direction loomed the aspiring new towers in the Grand Central zone. If the night were heavy these towers rose into obscurity beneath gray mists. Their tops caught the snow and halted it midway in its fall to the ground. The Princesse felt she had passed away and was now suspended in some fantastic heaven.

One day she hired a car and drove for hours around the city. She invited Niobe Why and Olaf Andersen to ride along. The driver was well-informed and pointed out the notable landmarks. The Princesse paid little heed, and concentrated on signs in windows. In Wall Street they passed an agency of the Home Life Insurance Company. The Princesse was greatly intrigued. "In a land where divorce is so prevalent," she reflected, "I suppose it is sensible to have one's home life insured."

Finding the newspapers so unintelligible, she decided to

try American magazines. The quickest way to learn about a country was to study its periodical literature. She told Mirabelle to go out to an agency and subscribe to some assorted magazines.

"Which magazines do you want?" asked Mirabelle.

"How do I know?" replied the Princesse petulantly. "Subscribe to all they have."

Mirabelle did as she was told. And over the next few weeks the Princesse de Villefranche received the current issues of Club Women's World, The American Boy, Western Trails, I Confess, Christian Business, Dogdom, Voices, Farm and Fireside, Beach and Pool, Trotter and Pacer, Hound and Horn, Live and Learn, Parks and Recreation, Singing and Playing, The Catholic Girl, Everyday Art, Creative Reading, Dental Cosmos, All's Well, Grit, Romance, The Swine World, American Nut Journal, Southern Hardware, The Bookman, Good Roads, Dream World, Ballyhoo, Motor Land, Kodakery, Camping, Bantams and Ornamental Fowls, Ave Maria, Target (For Boys), The Flutist, St. Nicholas, Liberty, Time, Fortune, Thrift, Better Flowers, Harp, Smart Set, Yachting, Charm, The Crisis, The Arena and Strength, Antiques, How to Eat, The Woman's Home Companion, Vogue, Baseball, Better Times, The Cat Courier, Radio Digest, Television News, Babyhood, Hooey, The Maritime Baptist, The New Yorker, Aw Nerts, Brain, Movieland, Hush, Opportunity, Forward, Our Navy, and Your Body.

V

A few days after his arrival in New York Napier Knightsbridge shipped the sofa on out west to April Overjoy. He
put Lady Rover's address on the corner of the crate, and
felt greatly relieved.

Already his funds were shrinking alarmingly, and he
spent quite a sum in sending an importunate cable to Pamela
in Honolulu. *Get Up and Rest* was doing well, but the
Matelot Mad number had been taken out. After the first
month, it seemed, it hadn't gone over so "big." (The explanation was that the patronage now was predominantly
provincial.) Thus Napier was deprived of even the modest
weekly royalty check which the lyric of this song had
formerly brought him. He felt that New York was mad
and exhausting, but very amusing withal.

A week or so later Victor Zukor rang up, his voice
sounding terribly blue. His sculptor friend who had won
the *Prix de Rome,* had gone, he said, for some mysterious
reason away to Rome. Mr. America was stranded in New
York and wanted to come around. He showed up at the
Shelton in less than half an hour.

"Well, old man, you look as if you'd been hitting the
pace."

"I have," said Napier.

" 'Glorify God in your body,' says the Bible," said Victor.

"I say," exclaimed Napier, "I've met a sculptress who's

(137)

looking for a model."

"Gee, I need a job," muttered Victor.

So Napier rang up Lenore Lanslide. "Hello. . . This is Napier Knightsbridge. . . I was brought to your cocktail party. . . No, I'm not a newsboy. . . Do you remember now? . . . I heard you say, Mrs. Lanslide, that you were looking for a model. . . Well, how about engaging Mr. America? . . . He's here in my room now. . . Righto, I'll bring him right down. . . He's really rather superb. . . Good-by."

Napier and Victor drove down Lexington Avenue slowly behind an armored truck. They found Lenore Lanslide working in her studio. She was wearing a long green smock a few shades darker than her hair. Her hands were covered with clay and a few small smears dotted the blue around her eyes.

"Hello, cutie," she greeted Napier. "I'm sorry I didn't remember your name, but you came the same day with that newsboy. And what a brat he was," she added good-naturedly. Mrs. Lanslide was never belligerent until later in the evening.

Napier introduced Mr. America.

"I'll strip," said Victor Zukor.

"Go ahead," said Mrs. Lanslide.

Napier looked around the studio, and the spectacle was astonishing. On a flight of steps stood the forty-seven models maintaining rigid poses. The space where New York was supposed to stand was marked by being vacant. Also a circle indicated where the District of Columbia should be.

The state of Texas caught the eye by being so gigantic. An enormous wrestler officiated as Texas. He was celebrated for his agonizing toe-hold. California was a tallish man of very vivid coloring. Florida, standing at the lower right, was a life-guard from Miami. Maine looked rather non-descript with sandy hair and gaunt features. Louisiana was tattooed in a very fanciful fashion. His abdomen revealed in red and blue an Adoration of the Magi. Above his right breast was the word, *Aline;* above his left breast, *Bobby*.

Victor Zukor by now was stripped, and Mrs. Lanslide surveyed him impersonally. "You're just what I've been looking for," she said. "Go up on that spot marked X."

Victor went up to the vacant spot and assumed the pose of New York. New Jersey kept casting jealous side-long glances, but Mrs. Lanslide told him to stop. She then went ahead with her work absorbedly, and Napier was quite forgotten.

At the end of the hour she cried, "Vamoose!" and the models came down like a Spartan phalanx. It was four o'clock and time for Lenore to prepare herself for cocktails. "What are you two up to to-night?" she inquired of Napier and Victor.

Napier replied that he was going with the Princesse and Mrs. Why to the gala opening of a new moving picture palace. Victor Zukor added that he was going to exercise.

"Some other night then," said Lenore, "we must go out on the town. To-night I'm going to Chinatown. Gin Sin

Fun is a hot Hip Thing, and there's going to be a Tong War. The Hip Things are starting in to-night on the Ong Bong Wong Pong Teong Tong."

Napier and Victor took their departure and turned into Madison Avenue. "Mrs. Lanslide is a very extraordinary woman, isn't she?" asked Napier.

"Somehow she scares me sort of," answered Victor.

An old man was walking ahead of them with a placard on his back. It read: VISIT THE NEW YORK VALETERIA. PRESS YOUR OWN CLOTHES FOR A DIME TEN CENTS A GARMENT. A Broadway address was printed at the bottom of the sign.

"I think I'll go there and press my pants," said Victor.

"Ten cents is about my speed too," agreed Napier.

They then started off across town to the Valeteria. When they reached Herald Square the air was filled with the fury of a fox-trot hymn. A new evangelist at the Glad Tidings Tabernacle was broadcasting a vespers service. Her voice, above the roars of an organ, filled the Pennsylvania Station district:

> "If you're sittin' in the dumps,
> Gettin' more than your share of bumps,
> Then get up and get down God's Word;
> If you're feelin' shot to pieces
> And your pants have lost their creases,
> Just get up and get down God's word. . ."

"In these cases it always seems to me more efficient to press one's pants," said Napier. To the strains of the hymn they walked down Broadway through a swarm of flashy

Jews. They went into the Valeteria sheepishly and took off
their pants and pressed them.

That night Napier and the Princesse and Mrs. Why
went to the opening of the International Foxy. Floodlights
illuminated Times Square as they drove up through mobs of
fans who were clawing each other, hoping to get a peek at
stars.

The lobby of the theater was endless, covering acres, and
combining all periods of decoration. The floor was con-
structed of wood painted over to look like marble. The
enormous pillars lining the walls were of marble painted
over to resemble grained wood. A spectacular gold throne
behind a malachite table stood between two playing fountains.

"What's that throne for?" Niobe Why put the question
to the doorman. The doorman did not know and consulted
an usher. The usher went over and asked the head usher
who was dressed in a uniform of mulberry plush and an
ermine cape and a tricorne hat with pom-poms. "A lady
wants to know what that throne is for," the lesser usher
told him.

"Why, that's the Information Desk," replied the head
usher.

"I might have known as much," said Niobe Why. "Now
that, Angèle, is the symbol of American efficiency—a
magnificent Information Desk and nobody there with any
information. Infinite machinery to accomplish nothing at

all. The machinery is all we have and what have we?" she quizzed herself.

Napier was looking at a lurid poster. The feature film, he learned to his surprise, was Robert Reindeer in *Lithe Limbs*. The supporting cast included, he read, Dulcy Wee and Pamela Woodley-Knightsbridge.

"Good God, it's Mother!"

"*Where?*" cried the Princesse, gazing up at the splashing fountains.

"She's going to be in the film," said Napier.

"We'll be lucky if we see a film at all," prophesied Niobe Why. "We may not even live through the Presentation."

The Prologue to *Lithe Limbs* was *Cavalleria Rusticana* condensed and staged as a ballet. Five hundred girls as Sicilian peasants danced the Intermezzo in flowing white gauze. It was played by a mighty organ, and danced before a backdrop of stained glass. At the end three thousand red balloons were let loose from the top of the proscenium.

"Doesn't it make you just *ache* to go to Spain?" said a pale plump lady from the Bronx to her escort who hailed from Flushing.

"I'm feeling ill," said Niobe Why to Napier.

Before he could reply, a "short" was thrown on the screen. It was one of the "Masters of Music" series, and dealt with an amorous episode in the life of Johannes Brahms.

Brahms was shown first as a bearded elderly figure conversing with an aged Viennese friend. A woman's voice across the street was singing his *Wiegenlied*. This sound made Brahms recall his youth, and promptly there was a flashback. Brahms was now seen as a pasty-faced juvenile wandering over Hungarian wilds. He caught a glimpse of a gypsy girl and seized her in his arms. That night he chanced to see her in the arms of a swarthy gypsy lover. The girl was clearly a wanton, so the life of Brahms was wrecked. As solace he took to writing songs and symphonies. At the end of the short Johannes Brahms addressed the talkie public: "Perhaps if I had had children myself I would not have written the *Cradle Song*."

At this Niobe Why had a seizure. "Quick! Take me out of here!" she cried. Two ushers appeared immediately and led her into the hospital. A fully equipped hospital was run in conjunction with the theater. And twenty-five per cent of the ushers were internes.

Mrs. Why was laid out on an operating table, and a consultation was held. The doctors agreed that the patient had acute nausea. "We'll have to keep you here six weeks," the physicians informed her. "The after effects of such severe nausea cases are being studied for scientific research."

"It's an outrage to make me serve as a guinea pig," Mrs. Why protested. "But it's just my luck to go out for an evening and have to come down with nausea. It's all the fault of that revolting Brahms shortie," she added.

Napier and the Princesse then left Mrs. Why to the ministrations of a night-nurse. Returning to see the film, they found their seats had been taken, and even the standing room was crowded. So they left, with the intention of coming back to see *Lithe Limbs* some other night.

In Forty-second Street they were attracted by the announcements of a flea circus. They paid ten cents admission and went inside a curious room. Its walls were lined with platforms on which various freaks were sitting, rocking, and yawning their lives away. Behind a screen in a corner the flea circus was in progress.

Napier, in tails from Savile Row, and the Princesse, swathed in furs, now gazed in rapt attention at a ballet of costumed fleas. The fleas were dressed in cream-colored tulle, and were negotiating a formal ballet. The Princesse thought that it bore certain striking resemblances to *Les Sylphides*. After the ballet a new set of fleas came out and played a football game. Another group ran a chariot race, and one flea jumped through a hoop. Napier and the Princesse were then charged fifteen cents extra for having seen the fleas.

Half stupefied, they walked around the room, observing its other extraordinary features. A blue felt banner across one wall was embroidered with WELCOME LINDBERGH. And numerous slot machines importuned them to look in on The Pride of the Harem. But the Princesse's attention was riveted by now on Jolly Ione.

Jolly Ione was the Human Mountain. She weighed five hundred pounds, and was dressed in a pale blue satin shift, with a pink ribbon tied around her head. She sat convulsively rocking in a gilded wooden chair. On the platform adjoining hers stood Little Jo, the Marvel Midget. He was thirty years old and thirty inches tall. Little Jo was wearing a dinner jacket.

Jolly Ione was exhibiting postcard pictures of herself.

"Can I buy one of those?" the Princesse asked.

"Boy, I'll say," said Jolly Ione.

The Princesse carefully selected one of the Human Mountain's photographs, with the intention of reproducing it in her book to illustrate to what curious size American ladies sometimes grew.

The next morning Napier Knightsbridge rang up Lenore Lanslide. "I say, Mrs. Lanslide, it takes a foreign visitor to discover things in New York. Do you know Little Jo, the midget, in the Forty-second Street Flea Circus? He'd be ideal as the District of Columbia."

Lenore went up to the Flea Circus that night and at once engaged Little Jo.

"I suppose you'll miss him, cutie," she spoke to Jolly Ione.

"Boy, I'll say!" said Jolly Ione.

Indulging a sudden generous impulse, Lenore gave Jolly Ione her necklace. It was made of clusters of pink paste diamonds which hung from a silver chain. It was found to be far too small to encompass the neck of Jolly Ione, so that lady clasped it around her wrist and wore it thenceforth as a bracelet.

One night in December Napier joined Gala Jersey at The Glimpse of Hell. It was now the spot in Harlem where everybody was going. This was the first time Gala Jersey had seen Napier alone in New York, for she and Racy Bumpus had become inseparable, and she assured Napier that Racy was her heart. She had found no difficulty in disposing of the manuscript pages of Proust. And Lenore Lanslide had bought the Cellini, once she realized it was for sale. The Chaucer remained unsold, and Gala made many appointments with librarians, which more often than not she was forced to call off because Racy Bumpus was so besetting. She was living at an hotel in West One Hundred and Twenty-fifth Street. By residing uptown near Harlem she figured that she saved many taxi fares.

Racy Bumpus dropped into The Glimpse of Hell after his own floor-show was over. He was jubilant because he had won two hundred dollars—half from the Clearing House Lottery and half from judicious betting on a Dance Marathon. Gala and Napier understood about the widespread Clearing House gambling in Harlem, but they had never heard of betting on a Marathon. Racy adjusted his several chain bracelets, and explained to them how it was done.

A Dance Marathon had opened a week ago in Madison Square Garden. A hundred couples had started out, but now only forty were left. The other sixty had prematurely collapsed. A gambling booth had opened up in the vicinity of the Garden, and two independent systems of gambling were flourishing. You could bet on which would be the final winning couple. Or you could bet on which would be the next couple to collapse. Racy had bet a day ago that a frail little pair from Syracuse would pass out before the night was over. Along toward morning the girl had fainted, so the couple was disqualified. Thus Racy Bumpus collected a hundred bucks.

"Why don't you bet on the Marathon, darling?" Gala asked Napier. "Racy could tip you how to bet—he has such valid hunches."

"I'll have to do something damned soon," said Napier grimly.

Racy Bumpus was so elated he wanted to celebrate. But what to do to make the night more festive? Racy thought and Napier thought and Gala thought and thought. At last they went to Racy's flat near by in Lenox Avenue. There they sat up all night drinking gin and playing phonograph records. For such, in the times in which they lived, was the nature of celebration.

VI

The Hoffensteiner Canned Opera season was to open New Year's Eve with Ambroise Thomas' *Mignon,* and the month of December was being spent filming this and other operas. After prolonged consideration Abel Hoffensteiner had found *Mignon* the only opera with two almost equally balanced soprano rôles—one for a lyric, and one for a coloratura soprano. The title rôle of Mignon was well suited to Armada Menace. She was on the scene almost all the time and had two important arias. The rôle of Filina, though somewhat less lengthy, was nevertheless more spectacular. It contained one bravura aria, the highly ornate *Polonaise*. This rôle was assigned to Utopia Lux who started at once to master it.

Armada Menace at first had opposed singing opposite Utopia Lux. But on second thought she had been reconciled with the prospect. She figured that a colored Filina would be so ludicrous that it would make her own Mignon seem better in comparison. So the shooting of the opera was progressing peacefully in the sound studio in Astoria.

One day Armada Menace was lunching with Wilburton Renegade. The secret they shared relating to the death of Baby Janet Basch was making this pair increasingly congenial. They lunched at the Casino, and Armada was enthusiastic over the way *Mignon* was advancing. She had recorded the aria, *Connais-tu le pays?* and had listened to herself in a preview. Never before had she sung so well, and she screened with flattering results.

Wilburton Renegade was skeptical over the merits of *Mignon* as canned opera. "I suppose they will jazz it up and call it *Getting Goethe's Garter*."

"Oh no," said Armada, "we're doing it with the greatest veneration. We've even had reproduced the old sets that they use at the Metropolitan."

After lunch Mr. Renegade went back to his office to keep an appointment with a new writer. A young man from Detroit, named Jasper Almont, was bringing in his first novel. First novels almost always bored Wilburton Renegade. And yet, you never could tell. Sometimes these young sprouts from out west had the real stuff in them.

Armada drove over to Astoria, prepared for a hard afternoon's work. They were going to shoot the spectacular scene of the burning of the castle. And Armada, as Mignon, would have to be rescued from the flames by Wilhelm Meister. As she crossed the Blackwell Island Bridge she hoped they would not have to shoot the scene more than once.

In addition to her work in the Opera, Armada was going on a concert tour; not in the flesh, of course, but in photographed recordings of recitals. Quite a lengthy tour was booked for her, and she planned it very carefully. Different programs and different costumes were selected to suit different cities: some Hugo Wolf and oyster-gray satin were chosen for Cincinnati; Reynaldo Hahn and rhinestones for Miami. Armada arranged her tour so that she was never singing in two cities at once. Of course such a doubling up would be easily possible and even profitable. But somehow it seemed to Armada a bit *promiscuous.*

One morning in mid-December she received a curious assortment of mail. The first envelope she opened contained a communication from an established musical periodical, which called her attention to two enclosed typed documents. Both proved to be pre-reviews of her forthcoming performance as Mignon. The first was a lavish catalogue of praise which announced that Armada Menace was one of the world's superlative divas, a worthy representative of the great tradition of song; the second was an hostile criticism which declared that Armada Menace was a mere pretentious upstart, a singer devoid of all artistic merit. The letter accompanying these papers informed Armada that if she would take a full page advertisement in an early issue of the magazine, the favorable criticism would be printed concerning her Mignon. If she did not choose to advertise, the adverse criticism would be published.

Armada was panic-stricken, and in a state of fear and fury she tore open three other envelopes, which contained letters from the various advertising department heads of Gargantua Gargle Incorporated, Kandy Kiddy Koughdrops, and Romulus and Remus Peanut Butter. All three made extravagant offers to Madame Menace to make a début on the air.

At a loss as to how to deal with such bewildering communications, Armada dressed and went out to consult with Abel Hoffensteiner. The impresario was prompt with his advice. He declared that Armada must of course advertise in the musical periodical. "It's an established racket, pet, like any other. You can't afford to run risks with success—buy it whenever you can." As to the radio offers, he suggested that she accept that from Gargantua Gargle Incorporated.

Armada blanched and murmured a jumbled sort of objection. (It seemed to her that to sing for Gargantua Gargle would be too squeamishly like a Borgia singing at a victim's funeral.) She complained to her impresario that a mouth wash seemed a bit proletarian, and that cough drops were decidedly superior and more in keeping with her position.

"Well, pet," said Abel Hoffensteiner, "if you feel that way about gargle, then better take the peanut butter offer. If you make a hit on the radio you may get a long term contract. Cough drops don't advertise all year—the cough season's over by March, and it's nearly January now. But peanut butter goes on all year, and you stand a good chance with it. Better work fast and clinch it."

Armada accepted the shrewd advice of her manager, and the following week she was scheduled to sing over station PGPG at ten P. M. in a big cross-country hookup on the Romulus and Remus hour. The morning of the same day she went to the broadcasting rooms to see how her voice "came over." Sometimes singers needed advice about the delicacies of going on the air.

A girl at a switchboard told her she would have to wait a few minutes. An orchestra was rehearsing in the broadcasting room but it would finish very soon. Armada sat down and overheard the proceedings in the glass-walled adjoining room.

A good-sized orchestra in shirt sleeves was rehearsing Beethoven's Fifth Symphony. The conductor, a young man, was complaining about the tempo. "Make it faster, men. The tempo must be quicker to fit the costly mike time. We've got to get this movement finished three and a half minutes sooner or there won't be time for the signature, *North Dakota Moon.*"

They rehearsed again the opening theme, the famous four note descending phrase, Fate knocking four times at the door. The conductor raised his stick again and expressed his disapproval. "No, men, you're still too slow. Take it like this: BOOP BOOP A DOOP."

From the elevator emerged a large black woman whom Armada recognized as the protectress of Utopia Lux. Mrs. Johnstone-Casey was going to speak over the radio that afternoon, her topic being "Good Taste in Decorating the Negro Home." She had come to the studio early to have her speech okayed by an executive, who now read it over carefully to make sure it contained no reference to death, no seditious remarks, no profanity.

"You'll find no contamination in mah speech," said Philistine Johnstone-Casey. "Ah'm simply making a plea to advocate the Directoire. Of course in mah own apartment ah do go in for Queen Anne. And ah admit in mah boudoir ah do give vent to mah own innate pomposity. But for modest Harlem housewives ah advocate the Directoire. Ah find that it's the farthest from the jungle."

Armada Menace was considerably surprised and amused that Mrs. Johnstone-Casey should be her associate on the air. Consulting a list of the day's features over Station PGPG, her surprise mounted into astonishment at the rambling diversity and general implausibility of its contents:

⌒ NEW YORK SEASON ⌒

7:00 A. M. Cowboy Songs
8:00 A. M. Gym Class—Doris Dove
9:00 A. M. "Greek Dancing Versus Tap"—Estelle Limb
10:00 A. M. "Swimming As I See It"—Winona Outing
11:00 A M. Renegade Books Hour:
      New Biographies in Brief Review
3:00 P. M. "Good Taste in Decorating the Negro Home"
      —Mrs. Philistine Johnstone-Casey.
3:30 P. M. Private Beauty Hints—Mme. Leona Horvitz
4:00 P. M. Modern Science Hour—The Growing of Grass
5:00 P. M. Karma Wombat—Cognomenologist
      "Alliteration in Nomenclature"
6:00 P. M. Fair Food Prices—Miss Anderegg
7:00 P. M. Polish Lesson
7:30 P. M. Girl Scout Activities in Winter
8:00 P. M. "Looking At Life"—Dr. Wier
8:30 P. M. Gargantua Gargle Hour
      Soloist—Baby Beulah Bunting
9:30 P. M. With the Debutantes
10:00 P. M. ROMULUS AND REMUS HOUR
      Soloist—Madame Armada Menace
11:00 P. M. Kollegiate Kitties—Girl Orchestra
      In "Ten Minutes with Bach"
11:10 P. M. "Italian Moments"
11:30 P. M. Wrestling Reports
12:00 P. M. The Two Dream Boys

Her manuscript approved, Mrs. Johnstone-Casey spoke
to Armada Menace. "Mah dear, ah want to thank you for
your coöperation with mah ward. You're an uplift, Madame

Menace, to mah race."

"Thank you so much," said Armada noncommitally.

"And ah'm sure your broadcast will be a real æsthetic little affair. Mah ward concedes you're a regular shark at *bel canto*," Mrs. Johnstone-Casey radiated good will as she vanished into the lift.

A man who emerged from it bore in his arms some grass growing in a chunk of soil. An executive explained to Armada that the grass was going to be heard growing at 4:00 P. M. This would be the first time that the growing of grass had been broadcast. "It's a PGPG scoop," boomed the executive, waving Armada into the audition chamber.

That night at ten Armada Menace was introduced to the U.S.A. "Good evening, ladies and gentlemen. This is Romulus and Remus announcing. You are about to listen to Madame Armada Menace who will render *Air from Louise*. Yes sir, *Air from Louise*. That title sounds kinda funny all right, but it's what they've got down on this program. Do not accept inferior Peanut Butters. Insist on getting Romulus and Remus. Okay, Madame Menace. Romulus and Remus announcing."

Armada approached the microphone and sang with a new-found confidence. Without any audience to terrify her she put forth the *Depuis le Jour* with increasing fervor and satisfaction. "*Ah . . je suis heureuse . . . trop heureuse. . .*" She attacked the top note with power and precision and brought the aria effectively to a close. After a group of lighter songs she stood aside and gave her place to the announcer.

"This is Romulus and Remus signing off. You have just heard Madame Menace. Remember the name—Romulus and Remus. Demand the ultimate in Peanut Butters. Remember Romulus and Remus."

A little bell then chimed and the nation knew that the peanut butter hour had ended.

With the money she received from her first broadcasting Armada bought a full page advertisement in the musical periodical which had threatened to do her damage, and thus was assured of one important favorable review of her Mignon. Whether or not the sale of peanut butter was affected by the whole proceeding was a problem which the Romulus and Remus Corporation engaged an extra efficiency expert to fathom. At any rate it was widely claimed that the cause of music was being advanced.

VII

The day before Christmas Napier and Victor Zukor went swimming in "the most luxurious swimming pool in history." The pool in the Hotel St. George in Brooklyn was so described by its management. Victor's entrance had caused some admiring glances, but no one knew he was Mr. America save an attendant who came up and said it was a great day for the pool because Winona Outing was there too. He pointed to a buxom young woman poised on the diving board. "Wouldn't you like to meet her?" asked the attendant.

"Sure thing, old man," said Victor.

Miss Outing, dripping after her dive, was introduced, and shook hands like the husky girl scout she had been before her days of international triumphs. "Pleased to meet you, Mr. U.S.A." she smiled.

"Mr. America," Victor corrected her.

"Righto. My mistake. I'm in sort of a fog to-day getting ready for my thirty mile crawl to-morrow." Miss Outing went on to explain that on Christmas Day she was going to swim around Manhattan Island "just to keep up her prestige." So many champions had enjoyed a brief heyday and had then sunk out of sight. But she had no intention of letting herself fade from public view. She said she would tackle Gibraltar in time, and ultimately Suez.

After an hour in the pool Miss Outing announced that she was going to walk to Manhattan. She asked Victor and Napier to accompany her, and Victor delightedly consented. Napier was reluctant, but Victor assured him that a hike would perk up his circulation. They walked up Columbia Heights in the direction of the Brooklyn Navy Yard. Napier remarked that he had been told that this district was more prodigal of irregular pleasures than even the waterfront of Marseilles.

"If you're so interested in water sports," said Victor, "you ought to go to Poughkeepsie in June and see the varsity crew races."

"They say Rio de Janeiro has the prettiest waterfront of all," observed Miss Outing.

Verbal communication seemed to be at such cross purposes that Napier changed the subject. He called attention to a building facing the river, on which was painted a sign with letters several yards high: MAN WANTS BUT LITTLE HERE BELOW BUT WOMAN WANTS SAPOLIO.

"That's just a quotation," Victor explained. "It's all in fun for advertising."

That night, Christmas Eve, Lenore Lanslide invited Napier and Gala and Racy Bumpus to dine and go out on the town. She was slightly bored by having Racy in the party, because entertaining a Negro at dinner seemed to her so outmoded, so typically nineteen twenty-five. But Gala had insisted prettily that Racy was her sugar, and Lenore had acquiesced with her customary generosity. Besides, she wanted to look in that night at a new club, the *Champs Élysées Verts,* and a Negro would be necessary to negotiate this.

Lenore Lanslide had arrived at the stage where she found Times Square amusements amusing again. For some years she had turned her back on Broadway, insisting that all the diversions in the West Forties were designed for the out-of-town yokels. Throughout this period she had combed the outlying districts of New York for every sort of bizarre attraction. She had frequented the Bowery theaters, the music-halls of Harlem, the Lower East Side burlesques, and the Sicilian puppet shows in Mulberry Street. She knew every dive and dump and den from one end of town to the other. And in her search for the ultimately exotic she had rediscovered Times Square. She now argued that the most fantastic entertainment in the world was to be found in the Newsreel theaters.

The bill at the Newsreel that night lived up to all her predictions. It opened with a shot of Japanese girls lined up outside Tokio, meticulously singing *My Old Kentucky Home* as practice in English pronunciation. Many other equally implausible sequences followed. Adagio dancers leaped in the snow on the roof of a skyscraper. Bathing girls paraded before King Neptune in a fashion show. A murderess delivered a confession. The Grand Duchess Marie gave out some opinions. John D. Rockefeller on a golf links in Florida sang a verse of *God Will Take Care of You.* Aimee McPherson was shown amid foliage in a tropical Los Angeles zoo. A lion approached, and Mrs. McPherson revealed that nowadays the lion seldom lay down with the lamb. She then patted the lion voluptuously and declared she would take it home. "And my word, what will the pup say?" the Evangelist concluded.

"Where else in the world could you see such a cast?" Lenore Lanslide asked with gusto. The bill over, she collected her various flasks and led her party around the block to the *Champs Élysées Verts.* This was a new Broadway night club which had a white floor-show but was under

Negro management. Philistine Johnstone-Casey had financed this unique institution. She resented the clubs in Harlem which, under white management, exploited colored talent but admitted only whites to enjoy it. The *Champs Élysées Verts* was her revenge. (Its name was a French adaptation of *The Green Pastures*.) The clientele comprised primarily the socially élite of Harlem, and white people were not admitted unless accompanied by a Negro. This was the rigid policy of the new club, and its business was already prodigious. The few white people left in New York who had no colored friends were going to any length to meet Negroes who would escort them to the exclusive new club.

Racy Bumpus saw his friends past the formidable doorman, and then he went on to Harlem where he danced each night in a floor-show. The dance floor of the *Champs Élysées Verts* was so crowded that Lenore suggested going upstairs to the golf course. The golf room was designed to resemble a Rousseau jungle, with artificial lagoons as obstacles, in which restless eels were swimming. On the course Amethyst Dudley-Frankau-Tingle was having a game with a party of brightly jeweled Negroes who were up from Philadelphia for the holidays. The black ladies who were wives of wealthy dentists and undertakers wore lengthy trains of lace and chiffon. The caddies were employed not to chase lost balls but to keep the trains from dragging in the rivulets.

"What a divine place!" Gala Jersey exclaimed. "They should not allow white people in here. It's too good for them."

"It's lucky for you they do. *You're* white," said Lenore.

Gala was hurt. "Well, I don't see why you accuse me," she said. "After all, I'm not responsible if my parents happened to be white."

"Awoos woos woos," Lenore was ending the discussion when something struck her in the eye. It was a golf ball which Amethyst Dudley-Frankau-Tingle had shot with exceptional vigor. Lenore could not see for more than an hour. But by four o'clock she felt able to stir, and Gala suggested looking in on the Marathon.

"Sure," said Lenore. "We've got to go *somewhere*." So the party progressed to Madison Square Garden and took seats in a lower loge.

Madison Square Garden was jammed with spectators who looked incomparably smart. It seemed to Napier that the women in the loges were even more elegant than those at London first nights of the Ballet. In the arena itself ten couples were slowly dragging themselves around. From time to time a man or girl would fall asleep standing up. When this happened the partner would administer a rousing crack in the face. This stimulus would take effect and the couple would shuffle along less wearily.

At the end of each hour the dancers rested a few minutes in their canvas tents. These tents lined the sides of the dance floor, and white-uniformed nurses were in attendance. Red Cross flags were blowing in the artificial breeze, and Napier imagined that battlefields looked very much like this. He and Gala picked out a couple which they found exceedingly attractive. It was couple number 5, and managed still to keep to a given rhythm.

"Why don't you bet on that couple to win?" asked Gala. The couple, though frail, seemed to have that quality of everlasting endurance which fragile-looking people are often endowed with.

"I think I will when I leave," said Napier.

From time to time telegrams of encouragement were read to the anguished dancers. A cluster of loud-speakers broadcast these tender messages. "Dearest Betty," read the announcer's voice, which for the moment drowned out the orchestra. "Merry Christmas, and remember we are always behind you in our thoughts. Gene and Clare."

Looking around the row of loges Napier saw some familiar faces. Across the arena sat Leslie and Salammbo West surrounded by the Cavaliers and the Plumes. The Wests had with them their three-year-old daughter Justine who, due to an erroneous impression of Lenore Lanslide's, was widely supposed to be a half-wit. When the child was two Lenore had tried to converse with her, but Justine had muttered only, "Glub glub." After that Lenore told everyone that the poor Wests' child was a half-wit. And the Wests, being highly inexperienced with children, came to believe the popular legend. They took the child with them everywhere now, for they thought it would not live long.

In another loge not far away Napier caught sight of the Princesse. She was seated between a young man and a young woman whose looks took his breath away.

"I say, there's Angèle over there. And who *is* she with?"

Lenore Lanslide answered. "The Van Dongens. I call them the Gold Dust Twins. They're practically Siamese."

"No, but seriously, who are they?"

"Shut up!" said Lenore. "I told you who they were. They're Fifth Avenue Siamese twins who don't happen to be joined together. They've never been seen without each other, and they don't spend a minute apart."

"Can they be met?" asked Napier.

"Usually not more than once. I've never even tried to meet them. God am I bored by Fifth Avenue people! They give me the woos woos woos." Lenore's bags and pockets were laden with flasks, and she had now consumed most of their contents.

The Princesse had her eyes glued on a dancer who was venturing an exhibition tango, and who was listed in the program as "Hercules Betty Batty." "That's it!" cried the Princesse, and Anna Van Dongen threw Miss Batty a five-dollar bill. The dancer put the money inside her bosom and returned her attention to her ice cream cone. Her partner, with one arm around her waist, was listlessly sipping an Orange Julius.

Just then there was quite a commotion over couple number 9. The man, Jack Wayworn, fell to the floor, and his partner, Phyllis Pastover, was raging. "Get up, you lousy slacker! Do you think I've danced in this hole a month for nothing? Do you think I'm going to quit, you cad, with only ten couples left?"

Jack Wayworn had cold water thrown on his head, and he stumbled to his feet. He clutched Phyllis and dizzily staggered to the strains of *With Your Charms in My Arms*. An attendant brought him a bottle of camphor and he misunderstood and drank it. This made him so ill he fainted away. The couple was then disqualified, and Miss Pastover had hysterics. The crowd booed lustily and hissed, and livened up considerably.

Wilburton Renegade arrived at the Garden with his girl friend Delight Wheeleright. They took seats in a loge adjoining Lenore's, and poured out a round of drinks from a silver flask on which was engraved the syllable MILK. "Whew, what a sport!" exclaimed the publisher. "I wonder how long it will be until we revive gladiatorial combats."

"Sooner the better," mumbled Lenore Lanslide.

"Aurora Overauhl ought to see this spectacle," Mr. Renegade added.

"I'm sick of hearing about that woman," Gala Jersey announced. "She's just like the Margie of Bert Savoy—so damned important but always off the scene. If she ought to see this spectacle why isn't she here to see it?"

"Aurora doesn't go out any more because she's decided that everything's going to the dogs."

"Sooner the better," Lenore kept mumbling over and over at intervals.

The Van Dongens decided it was time to leave, as the orchestra dispersed for an intermission and a radio was turned on. It was raucously relaying *Silent Night, Holy Night* from an early morning service. The Princesse reluctantly got up, and on her way out with the twins passed Lenore Lanslide's loge and stopped for a word of greeting. She introduced the Van Dongen twins who stood in identical poses. Annesley was dressed in impeccable evening clothes, with a white silk scarf tied around his throat. Anna was wrapped in sweeping black velvet with a white fur scarf around hers. Although it was morning and the night had been hard they both looked incredibly fresh. Their faces betrayed no slightest traces of either emotion or fatigue. Napier gazed at them spellbound, and knew then and there that something was going to happen. He shook hands with them both, and felt a curious thrill at the contact.

He suggested to Lenore that possibly they might leave the Marathon too. She pulled herself together and the party then trooped out, inevitably to Childs. Everyone ordered something different to eat except the Van Dongen twins. They both ordered coffee and cinnamon toast. They always liked the same things . . .

Napier opened several conversations with the twins, but they listened mostly and said very little themselves. Napier speculated as to whether they were really snobbish or only shy, and decided—because he preferred to—that they were shy. From then on he set out to captivate them, and after an hour he felt that he had made considerable headway.

It was now seven o'clock and Lenore suggested going to the Battery. The sight of the sea, she declared, was just what they needed to pick them up. The Van Dongens said they were far too tired, but Napier begged them to come along.

Lenore flared up. "Tired—at your age? Say what the hell right have you got to be tired? Come on, you two, get into that cab, and don't be so goddam Postum." The twins were so terrified by the sight of Lenore with one eyelid turning black through its heavy blue make-up, and her bright green hair rising dishevelled above the collar of her zebra skin wrap, that they entered the cab like speechless children, and the party progressed to the Battery.

On a bench in Battery Park Napier saw a sight which his eyes could not believe. There sat Victor Zukor in the early dawn holding two bars of Peters Chocolate. "What in God's name are you doing here?" Lenore asked as soon as she recognized him.

"I'm waiting here for HER—for Winona—the Girl of My Dreams. She's started at West Forty-second Street, and she'll be rounding the Battery soon. I promised I'd wait right here to give her this nourishment." Lenore could not get it into her head that anyone was swimming. She was in such a haze herself she decided that Victor was in a worse one. She felt unsteady on her feet but had no intention of going home.

Near the waterfront was a movie theater which opened its doors at dawn. It provided a morning haven for seamen and such who had been out all night on bats. It also gave nightshift workers an hour or two of relaxation before going home to bed. Lenore's one idea was to go to this movie, and she forced her party to go with her. Workmen and water rats and sailors ready for anything comprised the larger part of the scattered audience. On the screen an old revue was in progress with countless knees waving in unison.

One by one the party drifted off into sleep, only the Princesse remaining awake, her eyes and ears alert for Impressions. And when a ball bounced above the words of a song she lifted her voice above the snores and sang by herself delightedly.

At ten o'clock Wilburton Renegade woke up and wondered where to go next. Christmas was a hard day to kill if you were spending it on the loose. But New York was ideal for such a purpose, because at any hour of the day or night it provided somewhere to go to kill the time and conceal the pervading vacuum. More than any city in the world it was prolific of glittering things to do to drug one into forgetting that little worth doing was being done. He recalled that there was an Artistic Morning at the Hotel Plaza with Mary Garden as the featured soloist.

"Come on," said Lenore, "we'll hear Mary Garden— 'the pinnacle of earthly glory!'"

"Fancy!" cried the Princesse excitedly, and even the twins were enthusiastic. They felt reluctant only because they were in evening dress. But as they arrived in the Plaza ballroom no one noticed their clothes, for Mary Garden was making an entrance.

Mary Garden strode out on the ballroom platform with

a lithe contemptuous grace. She walked very slowly, and looked out over the room as if she were contemplating buying it. She radiated glamour, and was slim and more smart than the Rue de la Paix in spring. With a restless, imperious toss of the head she signaled her accompanist to begin. Some rare evocative utterance seemed imminent. Then Mary Garden clasped her jeweled hands, jangled her heavy bracelets, and the twentieth century's greatest embodiment of worldliness and *volupté* brought her rare incalculable gifts to bear on *My Little Grey Home in the West*.

When the morning musicale was over Napier felt he was ready to drop. He remembered the exhilaration of his swim the preceding day. It seemed to him like a week ago, but the recollection was pleasant. "Let's all go to Brooklyn to the St. George pool and refresh ourselves with a dive," he suggested.

"That's a divine idea," said Gala Jersey.

"Where are we going now?" asked the Princesse breathlessly, as someone pushed her into a cab.

"Awoos woos woos, what does it matter, cutie, as long as we're going somewhere?" Lenore Lanslide slid to the floor of the cab as the driver turned a quick corner.

"Say you! Go the other way!" she screamed, banging her bracelets against the glass partition in the taxi.

"Can't, lady," said the driver, "it's a one way street."

"Well what the—now listen here—you do as I tell you —I only want to go one way!"

∽ GOING SOMEWHERE ∽

VIII

Aurora Overauhl decided to attend the New Year's Eve opening of the Hoffensteiner Canned Opera. She was prejudiced in advance against canned opera, but she was willing to give it one trial. She went out very little to public functions now, though she was always hopeful that somebody somewhere might conceivably be doing *something* which was worthy of her exacting attention.

Aurora Overauhl was sixty-five years old, and she was living in a converted gas tank. She had moved into the gas tank as a protest against Interior Decoration. She was in the last stages of impatience with the contemporary decorating racket,—with Early American nests in the towers of skyscrapers, quaint Victorian parlors in Hollywood, Empire retiring rooms in movie theaters, and Queen Anne boudoirs in Harlem. Her gas tank which rose above the East River in the neighborhood of Beekman Place had no interior decoration at all. There was one big room with curved metal walls and no furniture except a piano. A spiral staircase led to a bedroom which contained nothing but a bed. In the remodeled lower levels there were the necessary facilities for preparing meals and eating them, but for the most part the tank was as barren as when the gas had been removed. An adjoining lot on the riverfront served as a landing station for Aurora's autogyro.

The recent retirement of Aurora Overauhl into the relative isolation of her gas tank was a *volte-face* after many years of active circulation. And it had caused as great consternation among her friends and followers as the Back to Bach gesture of Strawinsky had caused among the champions of "modern music." For Aurora had always been an ardent champion of contemporary manifestations. She had turned on the twentieth century the searching light of her observation, and had eagerly taken up arms in defense of whatever new phenomena commanded her admiration. After thirty years she had now given up, discouraged by the century's infinite capacity for vulgarizing everything of value which it had engendered.

Her severest critics were obliged to concede that Aurora Overauhl's life had been "brilliant." By this they meant that she had gone everywhere and known everyone, and had been conspicuously involved in everything that was going on. But they hastened to add that she had never actually "done" anything, that she had wasted her life in talking about what other people were doing. Her admirers replied that since she saw in a flash what everyone was doing and talked about it superlatively well, this alone gave her great distinction in a world which was largely comatose and inarticulate, and that she was invaluable as a human barometer which registered world symptoms.

But Aurora's misfortune as a barometer was that she always registered symptoms about ten years ahead of time. By the time the world came down with the disease she was registering something new. Thus to her the world seemed to be forever foraging on her past, and her life was lived in what seemed a perpetually premature and thwarted future.

On the perimeters of things she was always seeing small neglected factors. She would get excited and talk about these, and soon other people would see them. In about ten years everybody would see them and take them up and destroy them,—destroy them, that is, as far as Aurora's pleasure in them was concerned. Reversing the order of Midas, the world would turn her gold into dross.

Years ago Aurora had courted criticism by investigating Harlem. She had been one of the first to publicly appreciate the unique gifts of American Negroes. She had admired and encouraged their jazz and their dancing and their rich and inspired humour. But now she had lived to see these talents exploited and exaggerated by whites. White trash now flocked every night to Harlem, spoiling the native black "thing" with flattery. The Negroes returned this flattery in turn by the ancient means of imitation. Negroes were more and more imitating whites and thus losing their integral values.

A few years back Aurora had entertained high hopes for the movies. But the interests of big business had prevented the films from developing into anything worthy of her consideration.

With an almost breathless interest she had followed the early developments of radio. The scientific discoveries in this field were to her a modern magic. But she had lived to see the radio come under the monopoly of Romulus and Remus

Peanut Butter. In despair she had disconnected her receiv-
ing set and flung it into the East River.

With all of her early enthusiasms the world had now
caught up. Ten years ago she had talked about the poten-
tial beauty of steel and glass interiors. And by now every
shoe shop on the Avenue had gone in for steel and glass. Its
quality of patrician severity had been irretrievably lost.
Aurora concluded that engineering was one thing which
could not be spoiled. A gas tank was at least a clear-cut in-
corruptible cylinder. So into it she had moved and cut herself off from the life of the city. She refused to endure the
annoyance of a telephone and people found her almost inaccessible. If she wanted to see a particular person she
arranged the matter herself. No one ever refused an invitation from Aurora Overauhl, and the critical old lady was
growing increasingly arrogant.

Discouraged by the results of her years of persuasive talking, she now had concluded that possibly silence was
golden. In years gone by her vocabulary had known no
limits. On any subject which engaged her attention she
would give out fluent, often rhyming, pyrotechnical sentences, clause after clause falling into place, the verb being
kept for the end and illuminating all that had gone before.
But by now she was tired of giving her acquaintances this
species of entertainment. She still enjoyed talking, but no
one she talked to ever seemed to have much to reply. So she
now reserved her more impressive sallies of conversation for
herself. While arranging her hair in front of her mirror she

would often rival Landor in devising imaginary dialogues. Alone, she would pitch polished sentences back and forth like tennis balls over a net in a set wherein she was miraculously serving on both sides.

To the world at large she now spoke almost entirely in monosyllables, her sentences resembling a series of concentrated telegrams from people who were stingy and would not use more than ten words. Her more resentful friends were delighted that she apparently had lost her verbal facility. But as soon as they left her Aurora would light a cigarette and talk. Cascades and rapids and whirlpools of language would resound through the spaces of the gas tank. Sometimes her old servant, a colored dame named Meraude, would come into the room and listen. At the end of an hour Aurora would cease, and Meraude would exclaim, "You've said it!"

From her East Side retreat Aurora still exercised an ominous power over the city. Producers and publishers and exhibitors at galleries were deeply in fear of her opinion. For whatever it was it was sure to be repeated, and thus by a word she could sometimes make or break a play or a novel. A large section of Aurora's acquaintance, and this included a large section of the city's population, was incapable of forming any critical opinion until Aurora had formulated hers. In the old days when she frequented first nights in the theater, even critics would attempt to overhear her comments after the play in the lobby. They themselves might have found the play very poor until they heard her verdict.

But if she said, "This play was written by a genius who has no talent but nevertheless it powerfully invades one's imagination," they would hurry to their offices and write enthusiastic reviews which the producers would quote in the newspapers.

Aurora, who in spirit was probably less a "homebody" than anyone else alive, had been driven into seclusion by what she considered the dreary lunacy of the way her friends went about. Everyone she knew incessantly went somewhere, either to parties or to Europe where they went to more parties with the same people they had just gone to parties with in New York. This perpetual motion, Aurora decided, was a smoke-screen to cover stagnation; constant peregrination without destination was a drug which more and more people demanded because they lacked the necessary depths of self-sufficiency to nourish themselves where they were. As a living protest against this tendency Aurora had determined to emulate the admirable Miss Furr and Miss Skeene and "stay in one place and be gay there." Without stirring from her gas tank she could always indulge her mania for listening to music at home under conditions approaching in exclusiveness those of Ludwig of Bavaria. She could draw up elaborate plans for making America into a monarchy. She believed that this was the first step needed to bring glamour back into a world which longed pathetically for splendor. It were better, she felt, for America to go into its decadence on a red carpet with appropriate pomp than to slink into it surreptitiously in the basements of speakeasies. Bathing Beauty contest winners seemed sad substitutes for queens . . .

In addition to her passion for music and monarchy, Aurora's third preoccupation at present was flying an autogyro. It satisfied a need in her for flight from the waste-land of the earth in its present doldrums. People began to say that Aurora of course was going mad; that her insistence on hearing music at home was a manifestation of *folie de grandeur;* that her plan for an American monarchy was obviously idiotic; and that since she had little mechanical sense she would surely kill herself in that autogyro.

On Christmas Eve, alone in her gas tank, she listened to a Mozart program. She engaged an orchestra and Olaf Andersen officiated as piano soloist. He played the Concerto in D major, and throughout the second movement, the poignant Romanze in B Flat, Aurora Overauhl wept; not unhappily, nor even sentimentally, but from automatic physical response.

Aurora Overauhl loved music. This is not to say that she was what is known as a "music-lover." The country was filled with music-lovers, but only a few really loved music. Aurora differed from the general run of music-lovers in that she did not consider music an accompaniment to something else. Music for her was not something to half listen to during dinner, it was not a solace, not an expression of literary emotions, not a soothing quantity, not an aphrodisiac, not a relaxation, not a pastime, and not a substitute for anything else. Music was music. To write great music required con-

centrated, conscious effort on the composer's part in addition
to the initial "inspiration"; to perform great music required
years of concentrated conscious effort on the interpreter's
part in addition to the initial "talent"; and to listen to great
music, Aurora Overauhl believed, required concentrated,
conscious effort on the listener's part in addition to the initial
will-to-listen.

America was listening to music now more than any nation had ever listened before. But music now had less significance for its hearers than ever before in its history. Anyone
could push a plug any minute and listen to "good" music.
The overture to *Meistersinger* was frequently roaring in the
back rooms of German delicatessens. *Boris Godounow* issued
from shoe-shining parlors, and Haydn minuets were heard
in speakeasies. People were learning to dismiss music from
their ears in the way that they dismissed riveting.

Aurora had recently been antagonized by a speech, reproduced in New York papers, of a prominent British radio
editor. It began: "Broadcasting is the most revolutionary
thing that has happened in the modern world. It is as
though by the wave of a fairy's wand the loneliest may hold
audience of the whole earth, and feel the pulse of the universal life in bedroom or kitchen. We turn a gadget and the
dumb sky rains down music and song, dance and speech.
Bach, Beethoven, and all the great gods of harmony have
miraculously become as familiar as the kitchen clock. We
hobnob with the best society of all the ages, and our intel-
lectual and spiritual pockets jingle with abundance of

precious coin we had never expected to handle."

It seemed to Aurora Overauhl that there were more appropriate uses which a bedroom could be put to than to "feeling the pulse of the universal life," such as, for example, sleeping. And kitchens were designed to be places to cook in, not as scenes in which to wave fairy wands. The "gods of harmony" should not become as familiar as the kitchen clock. People should be obliged to make an effort before being allowed to hear music. They should have to go out of their way to hear it, just as they had to go to Spain to see the El Grecos. Aurora dreaded the day, which seemed to be imminent, when by means of television the El Grecos could be tuned in upon while one was taking a shower bath.

In addition to resenting the popularizing of music, Aurora could not stand to hear it reproduced. She argued that it did not sound the same. A picture did not look the same if it were seen through the filmiest gauze. And a kiss was certainly not the same if it came through the sheerest veil. In much the same manner sound was not the same if it reached the ear second-hand. In matters of sight and sound Aurora had become an intolerant purist.

On Christmas morning she was awakened early by a terrific din in the sky. An aëroplane was flying over Beekman Place disseminating song. It was ruining the morning sleep of New Yorkers by playing Amelita Galli-Curci's disc of *Home Sweet Home,* a hundred times augmented in volume. This was to advertise a new real estate development of "thatched cottages" in Westchester County. The plane hov-

ered around for more than an hour and showed no intention
of leaving. So Aurora got up and went out in her own plane,
mounting out of sight and out of sound. Her one release
from the current intolerable vulgarization of everything was
to fly into space which was uncontaminated by crooners,
comedians, and coloraturas.

Thousands of feet above Long Island estates Aurora re-
viewed in her mind her extensive acquaintance, and selected
Jasper Almont to escort her to the opening of the Canned
Opera.

The young novelist from Detroit had been sent to meet
her by a mutual friend the previous week. He was elated because Wilburton Renegade had accepted his novel for publication in his spring list. Aurora descended to earth and
sent him a wire inviting him to accompany her to the Opera.
He had made other arrangements for New Year's Eve, having a date with a Sutton Place débutante. But he speedily
ditched the débutante and accepted Aurora's invitation.

All the Best People attended the opening of the Hoffensteiner Canned Opera. The old Gotham Colosseum was "resplendent with jewels" as the Society editors pointed out.

Attending her own début at the Opera, Armada Menace
sat in a box. Her guests were Wilburton Renegade, the Van
Dongen twins, (who were opera enthusiasts), the Princesse
de Villefranche, and Napier Knightsbridge. These last had
been invited on the suggestion of Mr. Renegade.

Just before the overture Aurora Overauhl arrived with

Jasper Almont. She was dressed severely in various shades of white. A tight white turban was wrapped around her head, accentuating the chiseled outline of her strange white face.

Mignon began. The opening scene showed a courtyard of a German inn. Townspeople and gypsies were milling about in a muddled colored confusion. Armada Menace soon made her entrance and the audience was moved to applaud. At this the diva herself stood up in her box and took a bow which nobody saw. After the familiar *Connais-tu le pays?* the house cut loose and acclaimed her. Armada had won at last a gratifying metropolitan triumph. Canned Opera was her ideal medium, since she performed it alone in a sound-proof room in Astoria.

During the arias the sets dissolved and the singers were shown in close-ups. When Utopia Lux began the Polonaise one saw only her head and shoulders. As the aria progressed one saw more and more until at the climax she was fully revealed. She was dressed in pink accordion plaited lace and wore a tall powdered wig. Her chocolate cheeks and her throat and her shoulders and her bosom were all covered over with dimples. She attempted a slight dance movement as she performed the florid cadenza:

> "Yes, for tonight I am Queen of the Fairies!
> Observe ye here my sceptre bright,
> And behold my num'rous trophies!
> I'm fair Titania, glad and gay,
> I cheerily dance the hours away,

ᥣNEW YORK SEASONᥦ

Fairies dance around me,
Elfin sprites on nimble toes around me gaily dance.
Mid the twilight gray, 'mid hedges, 'mid flowers,
I blithely do dance!
Behold Titania bright and gay!"

In the midst of the ensuing ovation Aurora Overauhl got up and went out. She did not even wait for Jasper Almont who was unprepared for her exit. The applause broke off suddenly, and a few other people got up and started to leave. If Aurora Overauhl were leaving they inferred that the performance must be poor. In a few minutes' time the auditorium was more than half empty.

Grosvenor Plume approached a newsboy who was selling papers outside on the sidewalk. It was the same newsboy whom Roddie Oddbody had brought to Lenore Lanslide's party. "Did that woman in white say anything as she went away?" Mr. Plume asked the boy. He was having to cover this opening for a magazine and he did not know what attitude to take.

"Yes," said the newsboy. "She strutted out and all she said was 'Calls!' "

"Oh, how unsatisfactory!" said Grosvenor Plume.

"You're probably wrong by a consonant, buddy," Wilburton Renegade addressed the newsboy.

Aurora Overauhl walked around the block and thought the matter over. The Canned Opera was thoroughly disgusting. But if Utopia Lux and other colored people were getting out of their element and singing florid Polonaises in

grand opera, Aurora Overauhl was to some extent to blame.
She had encouraged Negroes in their artistic pursuits, and
if they were now going wrong she felt she ought not to
desert them. Poor Utopia Lux had worked very hard, and
did not deserve catastrophe. Aurora Overauhl put out her
cigarette and returned to her seat in the opera house. The
entire audience followed her back, and *Mignon* achieved a
triumph.

IX

Between the acts of the opera Napier had done his ut-
most to further his acquaintance with the Van Dongen
twins. And he succeeded to such an extent that by the end
of the evening they had invited him and the Princesse to be
their guests at the Beautiful Arts Ball which now was
three weeks distant.

People attending the ball were obliged to appear in costumes of the period of Catherine the Great. And the problem of procuring such a costume became Napier's major
preoccupation throughout January. He had exhausted his
funds and was borrowing now from friends. Billy Marvel
and Yvonne Débris had been sweet and had given him generous loans. And Gala Jersey had come to the rescue with
a liberal share of her commissions. But all this was pretty
humiliating.

Napier had sent frantic appeals to Pamela, but apparently she never received them. She kept moving steadily westward around the world and her mail never quite caught up with her. When she wrote to Napier she addressed him in London, and the letters were forwarded from there to New York. Her latest bulletin had come from Shanghai, and had been many weeks on the way:

"Dear Naps, why *don't* you write to your mamma? I'm at Shanghai now but am leaving soon for the interior of Siam. We're going to film a story that has to do with temple dancers. Dulcy Wee is being starred again, as she has lost a lot of weight on account of being in the tropics. Ah, the tropics, darling, *you've no idea.* On one of the islands none of the young men had an eyelash left. They had all had their eyelashes bitten off. It seems it's a local love trick. *Do* write and send me the amusing gossip of London. Has *Lithe Limbs* been released there yet, and wasn't your mamma divine? Love. Pamela."

On Christmas morning Napier had been too much excited by the apparition of the Van Dongen twins to remember to bet on the Marathon when they went away from the Garden. He returned there one day in the afternoon to see how things were progressing. Only two couples were left. One was his favourite couple number 5. At the opposite end of the Garden Gregory Gone and "Hercules Betty" Batty were still in motion. The former couple looked remarkably fresh after dancing incessantly for six weeks.

Napier went out to the gambling booth, and put forty dollars on couple Number 5 to win. If the Marathon ended within three weeks he might buy a Russian costume for the ball.

One night he had dined with Billy Marvel and another boy from the cast of *Get Up and Rest*. As they left the restaurant he suggested that they go into a Photomaton and have some amusing pictures taken. Billy said it would be fun, but he thought it was after eight o'clock, and that he and the boy ought to run along to the theater. None of them had the correct time. So the boy went up to a man who was standing in front of a clothing shop window and asked him if he knew what time it was. This man was a plain-clothes detective, so the boy was arrested, and sent to Welfare Island for seven weeks. Nothing could be done about it. The cast of the show regretted the episode, for the boy was "an awfully nice kid."

Another night when Napier was dining alone, a headline in a newspaper struck him: LADY ROVER LOSES FIGHT FOR LIMB—ENGLISH PEERESS SUFFERS AMPUTATION. The following week he read in a syndicated column of movie gossip: "People who read last week of the shocking misfortune of Lady Marianne Rover who lost her limb after being bitten in a taxi by a lion belonging to the Italian Duquesa Barocca, will be interested to know that Miss April Overjoy has recently been furnishing her Hollywood home with invaluable old Victorian furniture selected from the Pall Mall London home of Lady Rover."

∽ NEW YORK SEASON ∽

Lady Rover's attention was called to this column by a friend who saw it in London. She promptly sued for libel the eighty-eight journals which carried the syndicate articles, declaring that she was not as yet in the second-hand furniture business, and that as for the woman named April Overjoy, she had never even heard of her.

Napier had serious misgivings that April Overjoy would make an investigation. But the star never doubted the authenticity of her sofa, for she knew Lady Rover was a liar. Anyone was obviously a liar who would say she had never heard of April Overjoy. . .

Napier continued to go to parties and to look half-heartedly for a job. On account of his superlative tailoring no one ever imagined that he had no funds. Mr. Renegade offered him a job as a reader at twenty dollars a week. But this would not even pay for his room, so it seemed suicidal to accept. Napier was intelligent and at times even "brilliant," but there was nothing that he could "do." Many of his new friends would have loaned him money, but they were all so frightfully rich. Napier could ask Billy Marvel for money without feeling at all embarrassed. But it would seem preposterous to ask millionaires for forty or fifty dollars. So he drifted along, trusting to Providence and Pamela, taking aid in the meantime from Gala. The weeks went by and he dreamed each night of the beautiful Van Dongen twins. In his waking hours he tried to decide which one of them he preferred. Sometimes he even thought that it was Anna.

∽ GOING SOMEWHERE ∾

The Princesse was rapidly filling her little black book with a wealth of Impressions. Fragments and erroneous scraps of information were now almost covering its pages. She too went to parties almost every day, but she found time to prowl around alone. One day on leaving the Museum of Natural History (where she had gone to see a loan exhibition of Fighting Fish from Fiji) she cut across for a stroll through Central Park. At the entrance to the Park a gentleman stopped her and abruptly asked her a question: "Do you think there should be a Federal tax on cheese?"

The Princesse was puzzled. "Why do you ask?" she said.

"I'm the Roving Inquiring Reporter," the man explained.

The Princesse tried to think fast. "Yes and no," she finally answered. For her public utterance on a political question she felt it were tactful to emulate American politicians.

The man then took her picture, and it appeared in a tabloid the following day, along with the pictures and the answers of five other ladies who had been stopped at random.

"Fancy!" exclaimed the Princesse, tearing out the page, and carefully pasting it in her scrapbook.

She had many odd little encounters in ten cent stores and on Broadway. In a Sandwich Shoppe one day in January she ordered a sliced cheese sandwich. The menu read: "If you like the crust say *Rough*." The sandwich was tasty, and as she went out she felt she should do as the menu bade her. There had been no crust on her sandwich, but that, she assumed, was an oversight. "Rough! Rough!" she cried engagingly as she left the Shoppe. But the waiters were rude and laughed.

The Princesse filled her Tudor City penthouse with all sorts of electrical contrivances: sweepers, curling irons, toasters, and vibrators, none of which she ever used. Her favorite plaything was an electric egg-boiler which boiled eggs before her eyes. The egg was placed in an oval support, a teaspoonful of water was poured over it, a tumbler was placed upside down over the egg, and the current was then turned on. The Princesse was always amused to show off this strange device to her callers. When the egg was boiled she would put it away behind the books in the bookshelves. She hated the taste of hard-boiled eggs. Her pleasure was all in the boiling.

It was proving to be a delightful winter, and the Princesse had never been happier.

One morning in January Armada Menace rang up Wilburton Renegade. She had thought the matter over, she said, and was willing to write her Memoirs. Success had crowned her career at last, so now she could write about it. She said that she wanted to call her book *My Struggle for Acceptance*. Mr. Renegade asked her to come to lunch and talk over the terms of the contract.

A mutually satisfactory agreement was made, and after lunch they went up to the observation tower atop the Empire State Building. Armada had never gone up in a skyscraper, and she was curious about the view. It was a bright cold day and the outlines of buildings were clear against the sky. Armada and Mr. Renegade, both slightly dizzy, looked out over all New York. They were standing as high as it had ever been permitted that human beings should stand. Looking down was a panic-breeding experience.

As they leaned forward and gazed down into the street the same thought crossed both their minds. They thought of the *chute* of Baby Basch from the lofty railing of the *Lethargic*. Mr. Renegade brusquely took Armada by the arm, and she suffered a sudden tremor. Had the publisher's truce been only a smoke-screen? Was he going to punish her now by pushing her to her death as she had pushed Baby Basch? Had he only been waiting for a chance like this to torture her in the grand manner?

He threw an arm around her waist and seemed to be trying to lift her. Armada looked down into the depths of Thirty-fourth Street and let out a cry of horror. Mr. Renegade brutally stopped her cry by kissing her on the mouth. In the bliss of relief she returned the caress and fell back into his arms.

"I'm leaving for Palm Beach to-night," he said. "Armada, you're coming along with me."

"Yes, I'll come," said Armada, completely relaxed. "I finished *La Tosca* this morning."

On the sands of Florida the following week Wilburton Renegade proposed. Armada was startled by his suggestion of marriage, and asked for a day to consider it. That afternoon, as she lay in a sun-bath, Armada Menace reflected. What, she inquired of herself, did it take to make a successful modern marriage? Certainly not "love." Love was a biological footnote, she considered, quite irrelevant to the text of marriage. She had married once for wealth and position, but she never could do that again. To cement a marriage there must be a permanent bond between two people, a something shared that was stronger than love or money. And did she not indeed have such a bond with Wilburton Renegade? Was it not perhaps the exclusive mutual consciousness of crime which was the ideal foundation for contemporary marriage? As she toasted her back and shoulders Armada concluded that it was. And that night after dinner she held out her hand and said "Yes" to Wilburton Renegade.

A few days later the publisher and the diva were discussing plans for their future life. He announced that he must be firm in the matter of the continuance of her professional career. Armada leaned back in her striped canvas chair and let slip a sigh of surprise. So Wilburton was really old-fashioned after all? He would ask her to give up her career and devote herself to his home? Ah well, if he wished it, why not? She was willing. She had worked enough years to win success and now at last she had won it. She was nearing forty and after this year she would be content to rest on her laurels. Her art would be perpetuated forever in her singing films and her book.

"Very well," she said. "I'll retire whenever you say."

The publisher started. "Retire? *Retire?* Why, you can't retire for years. I would not think of marrying you if you did not pursue your career. As Madame Menace-Renegade you will be a spur to our sales."

"I don't quite understand," murmured Armada.

"I mean that in selling you to the public we'll also sell Renegade Books."

"So I am to sing great rôles in order to boost the sales of books?" she inquired angrily.

"Better boost books than peanut butter."

This was true, Armada conceded. She would break her contract with Romulus and Remus and sing on the Renegade Hour. Her Memoirs would be a Renegade Book. She would sing to enlarge its sale. Her ambition, she realized, was not defunct. "Right you are, my dear," she acquiesced.

The marriage was consummated amid excessive social flurry. A flamboyant new species of orange blossom was christened the Armada Menace-Renegade. And on seeing her impressive new name in print Armada set to work on her Memoirs. But after a week of racking labor with paper and pencil she was ready to give up the project. She could not assemble her ideas in sequence, and her long residence on the Continent had wrought havoc with her English vocabulary and her sense of sentence construction. Mr. Renegade smiled at her ruffled demeanor, and whispered, "There there. There there." He bade her not to worry, and assured her that as soon as he returned to New York he would see that she got a good ghost.

X

The Van Dongen fortune was so colossal it could not be
accurately estimated. Anna and Annseley, the orphan heirs,
knew that they possessed a reassuring number of millions,
but they were never quite sure how many. Their mother,
Infelice Van Dongen, had died when the twins were small
children, and they had been brought up by their father in
an expensive conventional way.

As soon as they were old enough they were taken to the
Metropolitan Opera every week on Monday nights. They
loved the red plush and dull gold of the opera house, and
the heavy yellow curtains which separated in a graceful
folding movement when the singers came out to bow. But
their interest in music as such was secondary to the aura
which surrounded musicians. Geraldine Farrar became their
idol and they worshipped her whole-heartedly. The adula-
tion of this singer was a major phenomenon in New York.
There was even an organization at that time known as The
Gerryflappers. Anna and Annesley were enthusiastic members, and the greatest emotion of their early lives had been
felt at Farrar's farewell. They were just sixteen on that
memorable Saturday when Farrar sang her final *Zaza*. At
the end of the opera Bedlam broke loose and the singer was
almost demolished. Flowers were flung from boxes and
balconies, and the diva flung a few of them back into the
demented audience. Anna and Annesley captured a rose,

each of them claiming to have caught it. For a minute or two they experienced hard feelings for perhaps the first time in their lives. They always wanted the same things or else things just alike. And in a case like this not even Van Dongen money could procure a duplicate rose from Farrar. This lesson in values however was lost sight of in the general emotion of the occasion. Miss Farrar made a speech of appreciation, and Anna and Annesley wept. They cried out her name which was laden with magic, and followed in her tempestuous procession up Broadway.

The next year their father decided that they should go away to school. Anna should go to Vassar, and Annesley should enroll at Yale. But the impending separation sent them both into nervous breakdowns. They had never been separated a day in their lives, and the thought of it made them ill. A doctor advised Donahue Van Dongen that his children were very high-strung, and that it would be unwise to part them since they found the prospect so upsetting.

It was finally settled by letting them go to Columbia University. Their dowager aunts considered such a procedure outrageous. "Columbia University indeed!" they said. "Are Van Dongens going to learn typing?" But the twins loved New York and were happy to stay there. They went through their four years of college and "commenced" with the rest of the class, a democratic gesture which was commended far and wide. They had made the acquaintance of several young students who won Phi Beta Kappa keys, but when these young men after their graduation became drug store soda-jerkers (the economic conditions of the period providing no loftier outlet for scholarship), the twins were forced to renounce their acquaintances because of family pressure.

After this Anna "came out" with attendant luncheons and teas and dances. But she did not enjoy the débutante state, and was happy only with Annesley.

At about this time Donahue Van Dongen took a vacation trip to the Bahamas. To save time coming back he traveled in a plane and was killed in an aërial accident. The plane was smuggling in contraband liquor as all planes were at this time. A government plane came on in pursuit, but the pilot of Donahue Van Dongen's plane was prepared for inspection. By pushing a lever he could open a trap door and let the bottles drop into the sea. But in his excitement he opened the wrong trap door and dropped Donahue Van Dongen.

Thus Anna and Annesley came into millions and ownership of the Fifth Avenue house. They were slightly bewildered by their sudden freedom and wealth which made anything possible. They were bored by bridge, by polo at Meadowbrook, by bathing at Southampton, by dinner dances, and eventually by the opera. There were no singers now with vivid personalities, and the twins felt a little unsettled. They were restless and discontented with things as they were. They wanted to go somewhere.

Their dowager aunts tried to keep them in tow, and Chloë Wilderness introduced them to her collection of dinner guests. But no one took hold of their imaginations and they relied more and more on each other. They wanted to move in a glamorous world, but felt they had "nothing to offer." Of course they had money, but they shrank from appearing to buy their way into anything.

They found the Princesse a pleasant companion and were grateful to Chloë Wilderness through whom they had met her. But Mrs. Wilderness looked askance at the things the Princesse was up to in New York. Dance Marathons in Madison Square Garden were not fit to be visited by Van Dongens. And when the twins told her delightedly that they had gone in full evening dress to a morning musicale at the Plaza, Chloë Wilderness consulted their lawyer uncle and asked if there weren't a law. Aristide Van Dongen replied that the twins were of age, and might need to sow *some* wild oats. And he was not of the opinion that disgrace could befall anyone in the Hotel Plaza . . .

Armada Menace was the first famous singer the twins had ever known. Everyone who was anybody at all dined at least once at the Wildernesses', and the twins had met the prima donna there. They were greatly excited by this first contact with the professional world, and they hoped to explore it further. They agreed in finding Napier Knightsbridge attractive. He was so good looking and so beautifully dressed, and he knew such amusing people. The twins had been frightened by Lenore Lanslide, and perturbed by Gala Jersey. But Napier had appeared to be quite correct, though in some things he said there were luminous hints of dan-

ger . . . They were looking forward impatiently to the
night of the Beautiful Arts Ball.

The Beautiful Arts Ball marked the climax of New
York's Society season. It took place each year near the end
of January, and after that Society went south. The ball was
given in the Hotel Plutocrat, and sustained an air of high
exclusiveness. Anyone in town could attend it who could
pay the price of a ticket.

Two days before the ball the two last couples in the
Dance Marathon were still dancing. So Napier pawned his
portable phonograph and rented a Russian costume from
Eaves.

On the night of the ball he called for the Princesse, and
she was an odd apparition. Dispensing with chronology to
accommodate a whim, she was attired as Peter the Great.
She flourished a sword and on the whole looked quite a
swashbuckling monarch.

They dined in state in the Van Dongen dining room
which resembled an armorial hall. Anna and Annesley,
dressed exactly alike, sat at the head and at the foot of the
table. Annesley looked like a fresh young Russian prince,
and Anna looked like one too. Their costumes of white
satin with a touch of ermine were of an identical design. (In
matters of dress their tastes coincided. They always liked
the same things.) After the sherry the Princesse lost track
completely of which twin was which. To one or the other
indiscriminately she described the balls of the Duquesa

Barocca. The Duquesa had given her Catherine the Great ball nearly fifteen years ago. But the Princesse reflected that America was young and would naturally need time to catch up. She was all agog to see what America's most pretentious costume ball would be like.

At eleven o'clock they drove up to the Plutocrat through a line-up of curious onlookers. They took along four bottles of champagne and went upstairs to a bedroom.

"But where is the ball?" the Princesse inquired, surprised.

The twins looked quite startled. "Do you want to go down to *that*?" they asked. "Almost no one ever does."

The night-long occupancy of a private room had become a tradition of the ball. In the early years private rooms had been rented by hostesses as depositories for wraps and bags and as retreats in which to replenish make-up. But under the régime of Prohibition private rooms were rented as places to retire to and drink. The day before the ball most rooms in the hotel were loaded with cases of champagne. Policemen were on hand to protect the illegal liquor lest people should steal from each other. After the pageant which was staged at midnight in the ballroom, it had now become *de rigueur* for the guests to proceed upstairs and drink. They seldom would reach their own private rooms because they would have forgotten the number. They would go into any room they found unlocked and the occupants would pay no attention. The night would be spent in ruining their costumes in unfamiliar bedrooms and baths. Some time the next day they would wanly disperse and depart to Turkish baths.

The Princesse pleaded that she would love to see the pageant and the twins were acquiescent. At midnight they descended to the ballroom which was filled with people who were all too warm. Everyone was trying to get a view of the pageant and no one could see a thing.

The plan for the spectacle was that Arabella Bushell-Basquette as Catherine the Great was to traverse the length of the ballroom, walking between two rows of guards who were all supposed to be her future lovers. At the end of her march she was to be joined by Grosvenor Plume as Orlov and by Roddie Oddbody as Potiomkin. The three were then to ascend a throne, and *God Save the Czar* would be played.

In her white fur costume which was the result of six months of preparation and a special visit to Russia, Mrs. Bushell-Basquette was nervously awaiting her moment of triumph as the Empress. But Grosvenor Plume, her Orlov, was too groggy to function, and an announcement had to be made that some properties had been delayed (by the traffic, of course) and that the pageant would be postponed half an hour. So everyone went back to the private rooms and opened more bottles of champagne.

Lenore Lanslide was wandering, dressed as a *moujik*. She was there with Leslie and Salammbo West but she saw neither one all night long. As she went upstairs to look for their room she crashed into Amethyst Dudley-Frankau-Tingle's. A number of Wooden Soldiers were lying about and Gala Jersey was a sad-eyed Katinka. Gala felt ill at ease with no Negroes at hand, for her own race seemed so alien. Furthermore, she explained, she felt low because she had just that day received word that her favorite aunt had died in England.

"Who shot her?" cried Lenore Lanslide.

"My dear, she was killed by an omnibus," Gala brushed aside a tear. "It does seem as if my family is having to bear too much. It's just six months since my sister had to lose her little boy."

"Who kidnaped him?" cried Lenore.

"My dear, he died of the croup."

Lenore Lanslide looked as if she could not believe her ears. She stood unsteadily, and finally said, "How funny it must be in England." Then, finding this group too lugubrious, she wandered out and started down a stairway. "I'm Stewed Descending the Staircase," she announced to the world at large.

At one o'clock people returned to the ballroom in somewhat diminished numbers. But by this time Roddie Oddbody was plastered and the pageant was postponed again. So everyone went back to the private rooms and opened more bottles of champagne.

"Fancy!" said the Princesse. "It isn't a bit like this at the Duquesa's."

At two o'clock the pageant was announced for the third time and the Princesse was almost beside herself. The twins had lost all interest in it, and Napier was for staying in the bedroom. But Angèle de Villefranche was not to be deprived of acquiring a new impression. So she emerged by herself, sword in hand, and sallied forth to the ballroom.

She found that an almost ghostly scene was being enacted there. Arabella Bushell-Basquette, as Catherine of Russia, was making her long-planned appearance. Flanked by the guards she pompously marched and was joined by Orlov and Potiomkin. But the regal spectacle was going unseen except by Angèle de Villefranche. All of the thirty-three hundred guests had passed out in the private rooms. The Princesse, *bouleversée*, went back upstairs, and was quite put out to discover that the bedroom door was locked.

XI

To celebrate St. Valentine's Day Amethyst Dudley-Frankau-Tingle was giving a come-as-you-are-when-you're-called-for party. Another purpose of this party was to announce her re-engagement to her first husband. She was on her way to becoming Mrs. Amethyst Dudley-Frankau-Tingle-Dudley.

The prospective guests were sent announcements to the effect that on February 14th, some time between noon and midnight, Amethyst would be giving a party. They were requested to stay in all day, and at an unspecified hour they would be called for. Whatever they were wearing or holding at the moment, they must wear or hold at the party.

At five o'clock a bus drove up and collected Napier

Knightsbridge. (Amethyst had chartered a passenger bus which ordinarily plied between New York and Englewood.) Napier was caught in his shirtsleeves, and this circumstance rather pleased him, since it enabled him to display his braces which were highly decorative. They were oyster gray, bordered with gold, and at intervals in red and black a Beefeater was repeated, standing erect at attention in an emphatically Tudor landscape.

In the bus sat Gala Jersey holding a copy of the *Harlem Tattler,* the cover showing Kid Chocolate with his skin a violent blue. (It was customary in Harlem periodicals to print photographs in blue ink, so that the subjects would not look brown.) Beside Gala sat Racy Rumpus clad in some negligible intricate underthings of a brilliant crimson rayon. Viadella Fenestra, who had been summoned in the midst of a fitting, was wearing a half-finished pinned-up evening gown. Philistine Johnstone-Casey was holding her dog, Ophelia.

Napier was happy to see Anna and Annesley among the passengers. When the bus called for them they had been taking a nap, and on awakening they found they had both been having the same dream about Gary Cooper. They were wearing similar suits of ivory crêpe pajamas, and Napier thought they had never looked so attractive. Mrs. Dudley-Frankau-Tingle, taking advantage of a casual introduction to the twins at the Beautiful Arts Ball, had sent them an invitation to her party, scarcely daring to hope they would accept. But still they might. All sorts of people

went to improbable places now in New York. The twins
were delighted to be invited, and they felt very much on the
loose.

Amethyst Dudley-Frankau-Tingle lived in a Mediæval
pent-house on the fiftieth floor of a new apartment hotel.
Her drawing room had stained glass windows depicting
episodes in the life of Saint Antony of Padua. As Napier
entered the room he saw Narcissus Cook, dressed in a black
dinner jacket, seated at a modernistic piano in a dimly
lighted Gothic alcove. She was growling her newest song:

> "I'm gonna get a bran' new Streetcar Papa,
>   On the pay-as-you-enter plan,
>   I said—on the pay-as-you-enter plan!"

Willow Plume had brought along her cousin who was,
oddly enough, a Humanitarian. He was wearing no tie, and
he looked around in severest disapproval. He spoke to
Viadella Fenestra whose pinned-up gown kept falling apart
so disturbingly that she had reclined on an old divan re-
upholstered in teddy-bear skin. "This sort of party is outrageous," he said, "when men in the street are hungry.
Sitting up here like goldfish in clover while people are starv-
ing below. Think of the Under Dogs, Miss Fenestra. Think
of the Unemployed."

Viadella contemplated a tin geranium. "What is needed,"
she started in, "is not more employment. It's only more
birth control. There are too many people alive by far, and
most of them might as well face it. What if they did get

employment, your thousands, what would they do then? They would go to work and marry second-rate wives, and have a lot of third-rate children, who would be educated in fourth-rate schools, and after work they would go home to fifth-rate flats, and change into sixth-rate ready-made clothes, and sit down to a seventh-rate dinner prepared out of eighth-rate tin cans, and then go out to a ninth-rate movie, and come home and read some tenth-rate magazine, and tune in on an eleventh-rate radio, and hear some mush from a twelfth-rate crooner, and then go to bed and make thirteenth-rate love. Now why should a first-rate person like yourself worry about people like that?" Having thus disposed of various world problems, Viadella turned her attention to her finger nails on which yellow violets were painted.

The Humanitarian had never before had the matter presented to him so flatteringly. "By George you're right," he said to Viadella, as he tossed off a Dry Martini.

Napier and the twins had retreated to a corner for the purpose of exchanging compliments. But the hostess interfered, and drove all her guests to the terrace to play a smart new game. It was played by throwing eggs at passers-by in the street below. If you hit a man it counted two points. Hitting a woman counted one. This discrepancy was explained by the fact that a woman, because of a more expansive surface, was easier to hit. Hitting a child counted half a point. If a baby being wheeled in a carriage were hit this did not count at all.

Dozens of cold-storage eggs were lined up on a gilded

sexagonal table. You paid a quarter a throw, and Roddie Oddbody was acting as treasurer. After half an hour, the limit of the game, Racy Bumpus was declared the winner. He had a total of seven points, two children, four women, and one man.

Mrs. Dudley-Frankau-Tingle then promptly presented him with the winner's prize, which was a painting she had selected from a recent exhibition. It showed a cucumber, a clock, and a cannon in an orderly arrangement around a head of Zeus. "Do anything you want to with it," she suggested good-naturedly. "I don't know a thing about art myself, and I don't even know what I like."

Racy Bumpus felt a bit at a loss. He let his soft eyes roll bewilderedly over the polished features of Zeus. "It's a honey," he finally said.

Gala Jersey was ecstatic because Racy had won the game, and she told everyone that it just went to prove what she had always maintained—that the black race was superior in everything.

The Princesse was invited to Amethyst's party, but she had made other plans. Lenore Lanslide had completed her monument, naming it *The Land of the Pilgrims' Pride,* and she had invited the forty-eight models to a jamboree on St. Valentine's night. They had worked for her faithfully, she thought, the poor devils, and they deserved a night of carousal. They did not enjoy much variety in life—they had stood in one position for months.

∽ GOING SOMEWHERE ∽

St. Valentine's Day was the birthday of Jolly Ione, the Human Mountain, and each year the Flea Circus released her from duty on this day. Little Jo asked Lenore's permission to bring along Jolly Ione. Lenore said, "Sure," and described to the Princesse the imminent jamboree. The Princesse implored to be invited to glean some novel Impressions. A group of forty-eight models would offer an unexplored field. Lenore of course consented, and the Princesse arrived at the sculptress' house at ten on St. Valentine's night.

All the models were there, with Jolly Ione the only other woman. Lenore herself had gone out to dinner and had not as yet returned. Two cases of gin were on the floor and countless bottles of ginger ale. There was an atmosphere of some constraint, for the models were shy of a Princesse. Two of them were boxers from Brooklyn, and were known as The Queens Killer and The Astoria Assassin. A third was a window trimmer whom Lenore had recruited from a Fifth Avenue department store. How he managed to maintain Praxitilean muscles engaged in his particular profession was one of those minor mysteries which nobody ever looks into.

Jolly Ione, in deep mauve messaline, sprawled on a white leather couch. The Princesse addressed her rather formally. She was under the impression that her first name was Jolly.

"Isn't this room attractive, Miss Ione?" the Princesse opened.

"Boy, I'll say," said Jolly Ione.

"Boy?"

"What's that?"

"I thought you said *Boy*," said the Princesse.

"Don't mind her," put in Little Jo. "She's got boys on the brain."

"Boy, I'll say," said Jolly Ione. The Princesse gave it up.

As time went on and Lenore did not appear, the models resorted to song. Arizona (he had been a Mexican sailor) sang a chantie which began:

> "Oh those barbarous girls on that Barbary Coast,
> Zoom, zoom, zoom!
> I could tell you a lot but I don't want to boast,
> Zoom, zoom, zoom!

"Go on!" cried the Princesse. And as the song went on its implications became increasingly shady. It eventually deserted implication and grew to be downright bawdy.

The Princesse's hearty enjoyment of this ribaldry released the tension of the evening. The general air of devil-may-care pervaded even Victor Zukor. The Princesse told him how much she had enjoyed his posing act on the *Lethargic*. And this so set him up that he poured himself his first drink of Gordon's gin.

"Better let me put something in it," said Oklahoma.

"One thing at a time," replied Victor, drinking the gin like a glass of water. In no time at all he was thoroughly lit and feeling a little regretful. "I've broken my solemn pledge

(203)

to never taste the blood of the grape," he said dejectedly.

"Gin's made of juniper," affirmed the Princesse, attempting to comfort Victor. In a desperate effort to relieve his dizziness he was doing some resistant leg work in a corner.

The Princesse felt obliged to probe the models for "material." Modeling had always seemed to her a highly eccentric profession. "Do you enjoy modeling?" she suddenly inquired of Ohio.

"Aw not so much," he answered. "There ain't enough future in it. It's better than bein' a stoker, but aw you know how it is."

Connecticut, who was of a scholarly turn, questioned the Princesse briefly concerning the Palace of Versailles, and asked if she had ever done any churning there. Louisiana discoursed on tattooing, which now, he said regretfully, was done by machine. The Princesse was greatly surprised to learn that the King of England was tattooed, and that so, as a rule, were all members of English royalty. It was not for the sport, but as a matter of identification.

Little Jo and Jolly Ione were exchanging reminiscences of their days on the road in the "mud show" before they joined the Flea Circus. "Do you remember," said Little Jo, "the night Jack Dempsey came into the pit and all the clown alley knelt down?"

"Boy, I'll say," said Jolly Ione.

"An' that old boy who ran the juice an' grease joints an' fought the duel with the candy butcher right in front of the starbacks until the jig band parted 'em beside the spit cloths?"

The Princesse was becoming distressed because she could not follow this conversation, when Texas, the giant wrestler, came along and lifted Little Jo like a weight. He poised the midget high in the air, and tossed him and caught him again and again.

"Hot-cha-cha! Hot-cha-cha," Little Jo kept saying energetically.

"Zoom! Zoom! Zoom!" the Princesse cried, beating time lustily.

The atmosphere was becoming hysterical, stopping just this side of madness, when Victor Zukor clutched his brow, and announced in a terrified voice, "I can't see colors!"

"Cats can't see colors either," observed the Princesse. "They live in a twilight world of grays."

"I can't see *anything*," said Victor, panic-stricken.

"Boy, neither can I!" cried Jolly Ione.

"I've gone blind! Help!" screamed California. "Help! Help!" cried other models. Little Jo told the Princesse to hurry to the telephone. He was too short to reach it. "Call up a doctor, quick," he ordered her.

"What doctor?" asked the Princesse excitedly.

"Any doctor—quick! In such an emergency look in the directory and call up the first doctor you find."

The Princesse opened the telephone directory and read at the top of the first page: "In An Emergency Dial The Operator And Say—I Want To Report A Fire—I Want A Policeman—I Want An Ambulance." So the Princesse said all this to the operator, and added wildly, "Zoom, zoom, zoom!" thinking that this might make things sound more imperative. The operator decided that someone was playing a practical joke and paid no attention to the call.

Lenore Lanslide did not return home until after one o'clock. She had been in Chinatown. And at dinner in a Pell Street dive Gin Sin Fun had asked her, "How are you at pulling a trigger?"

"So far I've never pulled one," said Lenore.

"It's all a matter of accurate control of finger."

"After pianists," Lenore observed, "sculptors have the best controlled fingers."

Gin Sin Fun slipped a pistol under the table to Lenore. "To-night," he said, "Ho Hum and Fo Fum must die. They're the leaders of the Ong Bong Wong Pong Teong Tong."

"Swell," said Lenore.

Before long the rival Tong leaders showed up. "Now!" said Gin Sin Fun. He shot and killed Ho Hum, and Lenore shot down Fo Fum. For good measure she let loose a second bullet and assassinated Llong Joy Pwong. Gin Sin Fun escaped into Pell Street, and Lenore raced for a taxi.

Arriving home, she was astonished to find that the house was strewn with corpses.

The following morning the tabloids bore the headlines: FIFTY FELLED BY POISON PUNCH——MR. AMERICA DIES OF DRINK IN SCULPTRESS' ORGY——FRENCH PRINCESS MIRACU-

LOUSLY ESCAPES. The Princesse had escaped with her life because she had drunk only her own absinthe.

It was a gruesome day for Lenore, spent largely with undertakers and reporters. But she believed with Oscar Wilde that anyone "who is master of himself can end a sorrow as easily as he can invent a new pleasure." When all the corpses were removed from her house Lenore rang up her bootlegger.

"Hello. Say, that was a swell lot of gin you sent me this week."

"Why, Mrs. Lanslide, wasn't it good?" asked the bootlegger.

"I served it at a party last night and all my guests kicked the bucket."

"Judas Priest," said the bootlegger.

"Now listen here, cutie, I want some more gin for another party I'm giving to-morrow. And don't palm off any more bad stuff on me either. You shouldn't do a thing like that to me when I've been your customer for years."

"I'm sorry, Mrs. Lanslide, I just musta got a bad shipment."

"Well, hurry up with the fire water."

"I'll have it there in half an hour."

The following week Gin Sin Fun was tracked down and arrested, and he squealed on Lenore Lanslide. They were both brought to trial early in March.

"What have you to say in self-defense after killing an

innocent man?" the judge asked Gin Sin Fun.

"I did it to avenge my Tong, and for the sake of the traditional honor which in my country I was brought up to respect."

"Guilty. Electrocution," said the judge. "And what have *you* to say in self-defense after killing *two* innocent men?" he asked Lenore.

"I'm a woman," said Lenore.

At this the judge broke down and wept. "The case is dismissed," he said.

After her acquittal Lenore was a sought-after guest of honor at luncheons given by numerous Women's Clubs. But she was soon bored with this rôle of heroine. And she decided to go to Buenos Aires to attend the unveiling of *The Land of the Pilgrims' Pride*. Gin Sin Fun was electrocuted on the day she embarked.

Her heroic monument traveled safely, suffering one slight injury *en route*. When it arrived in Argentina the District of Columbia was cracked beyond repair. So Lenore removed it from the group and nobody ever missed it.

XII

One morning Gala Jersey rang up Napier and said, "Darling, I'm going to be married."

"Oh Gala, what do you mean?" asked Napier.

"Just that. Racy has an offer to open a club in Chicago.

And I'm going to try to pass. I'm sure I can if I sit long enough under artificial sun rays."

Napier felt a momentary twinge of disapproval. There came into his mind the eternal question, "It's one thing to have Negroes for friends, but would you want your sister to marry one?" In some ways he felt like a brother to Gala.

"You know, darling," she went on, "we're all going to be swamped by the rising tide of color. And I think it's only sensible to go over to the side that's winning."

"I'll not admit impediments," Napier was indulgent.

Through his marriage Racy Bumpus hoped to win some sensational publicity which would launch his new club into prominence. He had seen in the newsreels recently some very remarkable weddings. One couple had been widely publicized by being married in a cage of tigers. Weddings in aëroplanes had been a bit over-exploited. Racy finally persuaded Gala to be married under water in a Harlem swimming pool.

"I always wanted to have the Wedding March from *Lohengrin* played at my wedding," Gala said regretfully.

"But Baby, we can't afford a band," Racy argued.

"Maybe we could get it over the radio," Gala was suddenly inspired. She consulted a paper and, happily enough, the Chicago Opera was on tour and would be broadcasting *Lohengrin* from St. Louis the following Friday night.

"But it's unlucky to marry on Friday," Racy protested.

"Darling, we can't have everything. We must take the Wedding March when we can get it." So Friday night was set for the nuptials.

Racy Bumpus in recent years had been so run after by white people that he had no colored friend to serve as best man. Napier kindly agreed to act in this capacity, and the Princesse was pressed into service as Gala's bridesmaid.

The day of the wedding Racy had his hair anti-kinked and Gala underwent a new permanent wave. Racy also took a treatment for refining dark skin, while Gala simultaneously lay under a sun ray machine becoming rapidly darker and darker.

They were married in divers' suits at the bottom of the pool on Friday night, a kindly colored preacher putting the questions. Colored life-guards and various attendants at the pool stood around as interested spectators. The extraordinary wedding was filmed for the newsreels and shown throughout the world.

After the knot was tied old shoes and rice were splashed into the pool. As the bride and groom drove off through Harlem, the voice of Rosa Raisa was heard from St. Louis, giving vent in Italian to the mythological woes of the Germanic Elsa of Brabant.

XIII

Niobe Why was not released from the hospital until early in March. Details relating to her prolonged case of nausea now swelled statistics which no one would ever read. Aurora

Overauhl had invited her to come to the gas tank on the night of her emergence from the hospital, and had told her to bring along any friends. Mrs. Why was eagerly looking forward to this evening, for although she had been in New York four months she had not yet seen Aurora. She invited the Princesse to accompany her along with Napier Knightsbridge. And Napier had asked to bring the Van Dongen twins who had seen Aurora Overauhl for years in public but had never been privileged to meet her. Mrs. Why consented to take them all, for she knew Aurora welcomed new people.

On the way uptown to pick up the twins and Napier, Mrs. Why sat back in the taxi and complained. "What I've gone through these weeks and months, you'll never know, Angèle. I've been lying there in that hospital in an absolute hell of loneliness."

"I thought it was *well*," said the Princesse.

"*Hell*, I said," Mrs. Why repeated as they reached the Van Dongen house. The twins and Napier came out at once and the five progressed to the gas tank.

Aurora Overauhl greeted them cordially, dressed in a black velvet reproduction of the white velvet gown she had worn to the Opera. The Princesse gazed admiringly at her strong, polished, distinguished face, and thought that in certain ways it resembled Fifth Avenue.

Three other guests were there already, seated on a ledge which followed the curved metal wall. They were Jasper Almont, whose novel *Fain Would I Climb* had just come off the Renegade press; Clarissa Goode, a singer who never gave concerts; and in a corner the Princesse was surprised to see her old friend Cerise, the Duchesse d'Èze.

The Duchesse was spending the spring in New York as the guest of quite a number of Countesses and Grand Duchesses who were living there in leisure on their stipends from recommending beds and soft drinks. "After all, poor dears, they are earning their living," said the Duchesse, indulgently explaining these conditions.

"I'm spending mine," said Aurora Overauhl concisely.

Clarissa Goode grunted in approval. She was a large woman with a strangely appealing face. At first it looked pugnacious, but her sudden smile was tender. Her expression was a curious blend of belligerence and yearning. She had a slight occasional nervous twitching of one nostril.

Napier noticed this nervousness and Miss Goode was aware of his attention. "Go ahead and look at my twitch," she said. "I'm proud of the way I got it."

"How did you get it?" asked Niobe Why.

"I got it from sniffing for dignity," replied Miss Goode a bit challengingly. "I've sniffed all over two continents, and there's precious little I've found."

"Imagine!" cried the Princesse. "Getting a twitch from sniffing for dignity! Do you mind if I put that in my book of Impressions?"

"You can put it in your pipe and smoke it, Princesse," said Miss Goode.

"I don't understand at all," sighed the Duchesse d'Èze.

∽NEW YORK SEASON∽

"Well, it doesn't require much effort, Duchesse," proclaimed Miss Goode. "Look at travel. Look at the theater. Look at Harlem. Look at cocktail parties. Look at the plastic arts. Look at newspapers. Look at magazines. Look at the condition of music. Look at the Four Square Gospel. Look at advertising. Look at the movies. Look at radio. Look at marathons. Look at the Canned Opera. Look at conversation. Look at literature. Look at Society. Look at Prohibition. Look at the whole muddle. What is everything in the world to-day but Gargantua Gargle glorified?"

"The American Girl is glorified too," observed the Princesse.

"Oh Angèle," cried Niobe Why, "you're *always* so irrelevant."

"Nobody wants anything," Miss Goode went on. "That's why we all get nothing. What do *you* want, young man?" she suddenly sprang on Napier Knightsbridge.

Napier was too much startled to reply. "There, you see," said Clarissa Goode. "You can't think of a thing you want."

"I want to want," said Aurora Overauhl.

"What a marvelous thing to say!" beamed the Duchesse. "I wish I had said that myself."

Aurora Overauhl refrained from quoting Whistler.

Earlier that evening Clarissa Goode had attended a concert of modern music. The program had opened with Ravel's *Bolero,* and had closed with the first performance of a new concerto for ukulele and an orchestra of air-music machines. "How typical of our times," declared Miss Goode, "that

(213)

countless roaring air machines should support the solo ukulele. Behind the dry rot of modern composition the ukulele is the hidden symbol."

"But you must admit," said Jasper Almont, "that the *Bolero* is exciting music."

"It's exciting once," agreed Mrs. Why. "But you get sick of it after you've heard it several times."

Clarissa Goode grunted. "You hear it forty times the first time you hear it," she said.

The Van Dongen twins were excited by the fact that young Almont had written a book. They had read a review of it which had extravagantly praised its "almost classical form."

"Form? Bah!" scoffed Clarissa Goode. "A novelist writing about these times ought to abolish form. It's all such nonsense to try to give form to an account of modern life. No one has any design for his own life, so how can there be any *en masse*? There isn't any pattern anywhere. People just mill about. They mill for a certain span of years and then they just stop milling. People in a book should mill about for two or three hundred pages, and then the book should just stop in mid air. That's the way life stops."

"Ah, but Art," cooed the Duchesse, "Art gives Life design."

"Bosh!" cried Miss Goode. "The green carnation has faded."

"Then you advocate *Naturalisme*?" queried the Duchesse.

∽ N E W Y O R K S E A S O N ∽

"Tosh!" cried Niobe Why. "Who could bear it?"

"Then what is there left?" The Duchesse looked utterly lost.

"There's nothing left," asserted Niobe Why.

Jasper Almont, uncomfortable young man, sat huddled between the opinionated ladies. "All the same," he contended, "I've had perfectly marvelous notices. It's my first book, and I've been compared with Stendhal, Tolstoy, Cervantes, and Flaubert."

"How revolting!" said Clarissa Goode. "If anyone nowadays writes a few pages that have a grain of merit he is immediately dubbed a Dante. And any stripling commentator is trotted out as a new Saint-Simon. Why can't they say the truth—that you've written a slick little book-of-the-fortnight?"

"One mustn't be too harsh," ventured the Duchesse d'Èze. "We cannot expect the young to be Old Masters."

"Why not?" cried Clarissa Goode. "Old Masters weren't always old. There's not any sense in making concessions because it's the Twentieth Century. e. e. cummings must realize that he's got to stand up against Sappho."

"That's it," said the Princesse, waving her handkerchief. She was vastly excited to be taking part in such a heated æsthetic discussion. It was the first she had experienced, and she felt that it must have been like this in the days of *Hernani*.

"Ah well," sighed Niobe Why resignedly, "we're all living in an off era. I often say to myself that we're just

God's gout."

Aurora Overauhl had listened in silence to the ladies' exchange of ideas, and she felt by now that she had listened perhaps long enough. She never took part any more in conversations about books; though alone in the night she often wondered what had become of literature. To clear the air, she suggested that Clarissa Goode might sing.

Miss Goode was willing. She crossed to the piano and adjusted the sleeves of a white turtle-neck sweater she was wearing. She played some scattered chords on the piano and unpremeditatedly broke into a ballad. It was slow and sentimental, with an oft-repeated plaintive refrain: *"I'll ne'er forget that night in June upon the Danube River . . ."* It was the kind of song which under different circumstances and in the hands of a different interpreter Napier would have considered slushy. But Miss Goode transformed it into a weird evocation of faraway romance.

Napier consciously listened. Who spent romantic nights in June upon the Danube River? Who spent romantic nights anywhere? No one whom Napier knew. The young people he knew in London got married if the match seemed mutually advantageous. Otherwise they ran around the world from Harlem to the Lido in pursuit of nothing more "romantic" than the indulgence of casual physical caprice. He had become convinced that romantic love was a concept which one grew up to believe in much as one believed in Santa Claus. At an early age one discarded belief in Santa Claus, but he remained nevertheless a well established con-

cept. Belief in romantic love was discarded considerably
later, but it similarly remained a thing one felt one knew
about. A poignant song about moonlight nights in June
upon the Danube River seemed to stir up some sort of
buried memory. And why, it suddenly occurred to Napier,
should it remain buried? He felt that at twenty-four he
still might recapture romantic illusion. But he knew no
one with whom he might conceivably share it except the
Van Dongen twins. He looked up quickly in the direction
of the twins and found them both staring at him. They too,
under the spell of Clarissa Goode's oracular voice, had arrived at a disquieting realization. They had just become
aware of a new aspect of the fact that they always wanted
the same things . . .

A silence followed Clarissa Goode's performance. There
seemed to be a subtle general recognition that a chemical
disturbance had taken place.

Jasper Almont crossed over to the Princesse and told her
about Detroit. He advised her that she ought to visit that
city because New York was not America. But their tête-à-
tête was broken up by Clarissa Goode. She had read in the
papers about Gala Jersey's wedding, and was interested in
asking the Princesse about her.

"I think her wedding was an outrage against *moeurs*,"
said Niobe Why.

"Well, I don't," said Clarissa Goode. "Negroes are sometimes complete people. Most people at present are fragments
of people and it generally takes half a dozen to make one."

"Fancy!" said the Princesse.

"It's true," Miss Goode cleared her throat and went on. "That's what makes monogamy so unsuccessful. You marry somebody and you find you've got only a part of a person. People should marry any number of people. No one person is enough any more. And no one sex is either." She lighted a cigarette and strode like an Amazon across the floor of the gas tank.

The Van Dongen twins had been almost completely inarticulate all evening. They had been electrified by the powerful silent presence of Aurora Overauhl. And now they were highly perturbed by the manner and opinions of Clarissa Goode. They felt so embarrassed by their lengthy enforced silence that they suggested it perhaps was time to leave. The gathering then broke up, as Aurora made no attempt to detain it.

As she climbed down the ladder from the gas tank Niobe Why sadly quoted John Donne. "How busy and perplexed a cobweb is the happiness of man here," she murmured. When she gained the ground she sighed again and resigned herself to a cab.

Alone, after everyone had gone, Aurora reviewed the evening. She liked Angèle de Villefranche and Clarissa Goode. Clarissa was a rare romantic cynic, and the Princesse was a precious wide-eyed child. Niobe's perennial grumbling was growing tedious. To Aurora by now even Futilism seemed futile. Jasper Almont was being spoiled by praise and

no further good would come of him. Napier Knightsbridge
was like a hundred other young Englishmen whom Aurora
knew but whose names she had forgotten. The twins, she
felt, were babes in the woods who would never learn to
differentiate the trees. And the Duchesse d'Èze was an old
French phantom who was dead but did not know it.

Aurora lighted a cigarette and started in to talk. Her
topic was one in which she was greatly interested and on
which in a lengthy sentence she felt she might bestow a
measure of her former pyrotechnical language: "Something
must be done at once," she addressed herself, "to accelerate
and facilitate America's becoming a monarchy, for the entire country is lost without a royalty it can look up to, and
the disparate denominations of the nation's population are
lost in concentration on divergent demonstrations against
Democracy and its foundations, and especially on the par-
ticularization that all men are created equal, which is, to
be sure, a palpable fallacy, but nevertheless an established
tenet in the citizens' conception of the Constitution, and
one which must be uprooted if the nation's action is to be
suited to its word—its action being definitely in the direction of the assumption that all men are *not* created equal
(it having long ago been dismissed from everyone's mind
that anyone was created free), and the means that America
is taking to demonstrate the superiority of a few mortals is
becoming something humiliating to contemplate, these
means taking the form of dance marathons, cross country
marathons, tree-sitting, bean-rolling, chair-rocking, pole-

posing, baby-carriage-wheeling, boat-rowing, poetry-quoting, Channel-swimming, beauty-contesting, strength-contesting, any kind of contesting, *any* kind of competition in ever-increasing repetition to advance the popular superstition that whether one be musician, magician, or metaphysician, one automatically becomes a patrician if one succeeds in one's ambition to overcome opposition and thus win easy recognition though one have not a grain of erudition, an effortless triumph worthy only of worms; and since the men and women of the nation form a rudderless congregation and out of their mental muddle come together in a huddle and sit holding hands and trying to cuddle in darkened, regal movie "palaces," and come out through red-carpeted, gold tapestry-walled, crystal chandelier-hung corridors into Marie Antoinette restrooms and lobbies and gaze about with their tongues hanging out at the pathetic, diluted, meaningless, gaudy, thrice-removed symbols of pomp and grandeur and monarchy and splendor, and look up spellbound at the trappings of queens (though Marie Antoinette be decapitated now and left to the mercy of intimate biographers), why not, since all this is true, why not indulge the poor souls' aspiration toward some material gratification of belief in *someone* of some higher station, and if Mary Pickford is to them a queen, why not *recognize* Mary Pickford as queen and build her a Versailles in Hollywood, or if Mary Pickford be too closely identified in the public mind with juvenile rôles and seem too childish for regency, then make Mary Garden queen, inasmuch as she can walk more slowly and handle her body with more regal poise than anyone else alive (these being two of the primary requisites for queens), or if Mary Garden seem too decadent and too Hunekeresque in her appeal to satisfy the commonweal, then make Mary Lewis queen, make Mary Nolan queen, make Mary Roberts Rinehart queen, make anyone queen, but make *someone* our Queen Mary very soon, for we are a nation lost in the night, without a God and without Divine Right."

She then went out for a spin in her plane and looked longingly at Pluto.

XIV

Napier now was seeing the Van Dongen twins almost constantly. Their real intimacy had begun at the Beautiful Arts Ball when he had deliberately locked the Princesse out of the bedroom in order to further his own relations with the twins. But their childishness had so surprised him that he realized he would have to act as abecedarian for a while. And this, he decided, was probably felicitous, for in addition to being so beautiful and so rich the twins were plainly malleable.

He dined at their house several times a week, to the considerable surprise of the servants. The surprise of the servants gave way to shock the night Racy and Gala Bumpus came to dine. "Dear Holy Father, it's a *coon*!" exclaimed the cook. Old Leopatra Pratt had cooked for the twins since they were infants.

After dinner that night Racy felt exhilarated and said he would do a dance. He took up a cane and went through a routine of frenzied anatomical dislocations to *Szerntnek Majus Ejszakakon,* an Hungarian disc which chanced to be on the phonograph. "Glory be to God and Saint Patrick," whispered Leopatra Pratt from behind a screen. She shook her head despairingly and crossed herself many times, for the sight she saw was to her an unmistakable sign of the end of the world. She perplexedly climbed upstairs to bed to the strains of *Ket Gtongye Volt a Falunak.*

Day after day Napier spent with the twins describing the pleasures of Europe. And he came to represent to them the glamour of all the "Old World" capitals. He was distressed by the twins' ignorance of certain Continental institutions which seemed to him like the foundations of civilization itself. The Sitwells, for example. Or the defunct Ballet Russe. They were innocent of both its history and its personnel, and Napier took it upon himself to remedy this defect. Throughout the following week he rhapsodized about the Ballet, and impressed on the twins' imagination the effulgent names of the dancers. And these names were enough to suggest to them a far off, drug-like enchantment.

After exhausting the Ballet Russe as a topic, Napier went on to others. He painted for the twins endless verbal pictures of the more picturesque personalities of London and Paris, some of whom he had met, though others he knew only by sight. The twins were absorbed by his account of a lecture the unearthly Gertrude Stein had given at Cambridge, which Napier and Anthony Stowitts had motored up to hear.

As well as with Napier, the twins were falling in love with the names of people and places. "Gertrude Stein," they said, "is she a Dutch girl?"

Napier was really shocked to learn that they had never read Miss Stein, and he asked them what for instance they did read. They replied that at present they were midway in *Jude the Obscure*.

With difficulty Napier controlled his impatience. And that night he drew up a list of books for the twins to read at once. The books were predominantly French, and their tone was not predominantly healthy. *Monsieur Vénus* headed the list which closed with *Les Enfants Terribles*.

The twins immediately ordered these books and sat up nights to read them. And soon they both were seized with a consuming need to go to Europe. Napier himself was preparing to sail, for the six months sojourn in America which he was permitted as a British visitor was drawing to a close.

"We three might sail together," the twins suggested.

"It's too bad," said Napier, "that we can't all three get married in the way that crazy Clarissa Goode suggested."

The twins considered this proposal very seriously. "Do you suppose that Uncle Aristide could fix it up?" they asked. "He can always find some legal loophole somewhere."

Napier was startled by this turn of events. Marriage was more than even he had hoped for. But he went with the twins to consult their uncle who was a widely known criminal lawyer. Was there not, they asked him, some obscure by-law in which it was implied that twins were *one*?

Aristide Van Dongen replied in the negative. According to American law two twins were separate and distinct entities, neither one being bound by or responsible for the acts of the other. Each carried his own separate moral responsibilities and obligations. In neither wills nor marriage contracts could they sign their names as one. And these rulings held, as far as he knew, throughout the civilized world.

The twins were crestfallen, and Napier too was deeply disappointed. They spent that evening dejectedly, reading *L'Immoraliste* aloud.

But only a day and the world was changed, when a letter arrived from Pamela:

> "Graustark, March 1
>
> Dear Naps, you vicious angel you, have you forgotten your mamma entirely? Here it is spring, and I've not had a word from you all winter. I thought surely I'd find some mail in Persia, but I didn't.
>
> We are now in Graustark to film a romance on the historic ground itself. Our directors believe that after

so much sophistication in the films the fans will welcome a return to passion of an Elinor Glynnish sort.
And we're all convinced that since *art nouveau* is now
such old hat there will be a hectic revival of tiger skins
and roses, and we want to sort of anticipate the movement. How true it is about the Eternal Return—was it
Nietzsche or Newton who discovered it?

It's divine here, and we have made a few trips over
into Trans-Urania on location. The landscape there is
more passionate. It is a little kingdom, just north of
Graustark, and not much bigger than Monaco. The
people there have some very picturesque customs. One
is that they marry in groups of three instead of in pairs.
The members of the family are known as the husband,
the hus, and the wifeband, and they say that divorce is practically unknown. It seems the present king
inaugurated this custom in order to accommodate himself. He gave a reception for Robert Reindeer and
Dulcy Wee, and I thought he was divine. He was educated in Paris, and he goes by the title of Henri III.
Robert said this was a curious coincidence, but I don't
know what he meant. Sometimes I feel almost il-
literate, but this winter has been quite an education.
How true it is so few of us know how the other half
live.

I do long for news of London. *Please* write me here
care of Cooks. I may see you in England soon unless
Dulcy decides to go to Egypt and do the life of

Cleopatra. She is reluctant because she thinks the public prefers romance to history. Anyway, how is your
money holding out? And is the pound still vacillating?
Love.

Pamela.

P.S. In the Graustark film I'm cast as a Balkan queen.
Quite a mischievous old thing and they say I'm perfect."

Napier showed this letter to the twins and exclaimed,
"We must go to Trans-Urania at once." They agreed, and
plans were made immediately for sailing. The twins then
sent a formal announcement to the Society editor of the
Times: "Anna and Annesley Van Dongen announce their
engagement to Napier Knightsbridge of London, England.
Mr. and Miss Van Dongen and Mr. Knightsbridge, who
has been spending the winter in New York, will sail next
week for Paris where the bride will select her *trousseau.* The
marriage will take place in the Balkan peninsula on a date
which is still unsettled."

When the dowager Van Dongen aunts read this item
they unanimously fainted away. And Chloë Wilderness
wrote a flurried, fruitless plea to the pope. But nothing could
be done to curb the twins who were of age and possessed of
millions.

In spite of the fact that from now on he need have no
worry about funds, Napier could not forget that he had
bet forty dollars on the Dance Marathon. The day he

sailed he looked in at Madison Square Garden and found two couples still dancing determinedly. The two men had gone mad, and from time to time in an imbecile way they nibbled at potted palms. Both the girls however had put on weight, and were out to dance to the death. The orchestra, bedraggled and hollow-eyed, was thumping out the thread-bare tune of *Without You What Would I Do?* Napier felt faint and rushed out into the air. It was thus he took leave of America.

The twins were so impatient to get to Europe that they chartered a spacious suite on the *Athletic,* the fastest ship afloat. On their first night in Paris Napier and Anna and Annesley went to the Théatre Mogador and saw a new musical comedy called *Lune de Virginie de L'Ouest.* This proved to be a version of *West Virginia Moon* which they had seen their last night in New York. This made them feel that the merits of speed were possibly over-rated.

After the theater they were going to visit the Mont-parnasse *boîtes,* and as Anna was wearing a wrap of black velvet which reached only from her shoulders to her shoul-der blades, she decided to stop at her hotel and change to more appropriate slumming clothes. Annesley stopped with her, and they both were to meet Napier later at the *Dôme.*

Sipping an *amourette* at the *Dôme,* Napier saw at the bar a bronzed young man whose face looked fairly familiar. He was standing beside a brightly dressed woman who carried a parrot on her shoulder. The young man, Napier realized at length, was Robert Reindeer. And a moment later he divined that the woman was Pamela.

"Mother!" he cried.

"Naps! Of all places to run into my precious angel! When did you come over, darling? And how are things in London?"

"I've no idea, darling. I've just arrived from America."

"Don't be so silly," said Pamela. "I'm really famished for news of London. I've not had a scrap of mail for months."

"But I've been in America all winter, and I'm now engaged to be married."

"You! How you do go on! I'm dying to talk about London with you, but I'm taking the midnight train to Barcelona with Robert Reindeer. We're going to film *The Bible in Spain,* with Robert as George Borrow. All the prima donnas who have ever sung Carmen are being engaged for the Technicolor choruses. We gave up Cleopatra as too hackneyed. My dear, the public is *clamoring* for novelty."

"Oh Pamela, can't you stay in Paris overnight? I want you to meet the twins I'm going to marry. They'll be here in half an hour, and they're really rather sweet."

"Don't be so silly," said Pamela again. "It's awfully annoying of you. But you do look rather an angel in that suit. What plaits and creases! However can you afford them?"

"I've been given a dowry. *I'm frightfully rich.* I'm going to Trans-Urania to be married," Napier was breathless.

"It was divine there," said Pamela. But Robert Reindeer

had looked at his wrist-watch and was whisking her away. "Don't be so silly," she called over her shoulder. "You go on even worse than you used to."

"But all of it is true—I *have* been in America—and I *am* engaged—and *oh so frightfully rich!*"

"Don't be so silly," the parrot kept screeching, as Pamela drove up the Boulevard Raspail in a cab with The Boy Friend Of All.

XV

On the insistence of Jasper Almont, the Princesse made up her mind to visit Detroit. After a brief stay in the Middle Western city she was going to return to France to spend the summer giving final shape to her Impressions. She had already sent some introductory chapters to her publisher, and was eagerly awaiting his comment on her material and her style.

Young Almont himself was leaving for Detroit to pay a visit to his family. With the Princesse he consulted a railroad time-table and found that a fast train to Detroit left at 4:15 P. M.

"Let me see," said Jasper Almont, "will that be 3:15 or 5:15?"

"Why won't it be 4:15?" asked the Princesse.

"Oh no, it's always different because they save the daylight. Now, 4:15 in the time-table means 5:15 in New

York, and that makes it 3:15 in Detroit—or is it 2:15 in Detroit?"

"Imagine!" cried the Princesse, lost in confusion.

They made the train by arriving at the station an hour too early. One article which she had received by post that morning the Princesse could not accommodate in her bags, so she carried it in her arms as a separate parcel. It was a sealed Virginia ham. The Princesse had delightedly subscribed to receive the Ham-of-the-Month, which was sent from Virginia twelve times a year to subscribers.

In Detroit the Princesse attended a barn dance which was sponsored by a motor magnate, and waved her handkerchief gaily when she heard *Pop Goes the Weasel*. The following night she paid a visit to the River Rouge Ford Factory and was driven through the various buildings over an indoor motor runway. She got out of the car to inspect more closely a most spectacular scene, where workmen were doggedly guiding pipes of red hot steel through shallow grooves. Absorbed, the Princesse watched for half an hour. Then she raised her voice and called aloud to a workman.

"I say," she cried, "do you do just that all night?"

"I've done just this all night every night for sixteen years," he answered.

"Fancy!" exclaimed the Princesse, driving away, depressed. The next day Jasper Almont called at her hotel and found her still dejected. To divert her he suggested that she come for a drive in his car which he had left at the door. The Princesse agreed, and at the last minute decided to take

～ NEW YORK SEASON ～

Albertine Disparue. The gloomy old cat was ill at ease in the unfamiliar hotel suite, so the Princesse tucked her into her box and placed it in the back seat of the motor.

Young Almont announced that the new Detroit sky-line was impressive when seen from across the river in Windsor. They drove across a bridge and along a parkway which flanked the Canadian border. They took some tea at a "re-freshment stand," and at dusk returned to Detroit. At the end of the bridge an inspector stopped them to search for contraband liquor.

"Got any booze in there?" inquired the agent.

The Princesse was indignant. Was she, a Princesse of the line of Villefranche, to be humiliatingly searched for "booze?"

"Mais non, pas du tout," she replied, speaking French, because it seemed more worthy of her station.

"Don't pull the me-no-speaka-English line. Whatcha got back there in that box?" said the agent aggressively.

The Princesse was alarmed. "A cat," she murmured nervously.

"A *cat,* huh?" said the agent. "Been over to Canada an' comin' back with some good old 1895 cat!"

"1925," the Princesse corrected him.

"Oh yeah? Well, we'll see. Open up that box."

"N'ouvrez-pas cette boîte!" exclaimed the Princesse. "If you open that box *Albertine Disparue* will jump out and I couldn't bear to lose her."

"Hold on," sneered the agent. "I'm gonna open that box,

(231)

old girl, or know the reason why."

Jasper Almont, disgusted, released his clutch and started to drive away. So the agent obeyed his government's orders, and shot with a skilful aim. The volley cracked and resounded over the murky stretches of the river, disturbing the drowsy fowls in Belle Isle Park.

As his final act in life Jasper Almont put on the brake. The car careened crazily to the curb and came to a sudden stop. The Princesse had not taken in the situation when another, still more stunning, imposed itself. Through a haze she heard another shot and saw the prohibition agent topple over. In a trice a strange man was in the car, throwing Jasper Almont's body into the back compartment, and seating himself at the wheel. The Princesse was speechless with bewilderment.

"Well, I gave him his," said the man.

"His *what?*" asked the Princesse, understanding nothing.

Making no reply, the strange man started to drive ahead. The sound of the shots had dispersed the pedestrians who had run from the scene in fright. The Princesse in confusion noticed only one thing—that the man wore a bright pink sweater.

Before the car could get under way another car approached from behind it. Three men were seated inside this car, and one of them held a gun. He raised it calmly and promptly shot the man in the bright pink sweater. The Princesse took note through a mental fog that this killer wore a bright blue sweater. In what seemed like less than no time, this new killer was inside her car, tossing the first killer's body into the back seat, and starting to drive ahead. The Princesse was beside herself, and she felt that she ought to scream.

"Take it easy, sister," said the young man in the blue sweater. "I did that just to help you. I saw 'em get your little kid brother."

The young man's voice was so gentle and sympathetic, the Princesse felt a moment's reassurance. "But—you don't understand—" she began in a shaking voice.

"I understand all right. Don't I just? They always try to get your little kid brother. They got mine last year. Poor little Dick. They mowed him down on the Fourth of July —the rats!"

"The *rats?*" the Princesse echoed in amazement.

"Yeah—the Pink Gang. We Indigoes are goin' after 'em hot."

It was all beyond the Princesse's comprehension.

"Well, sister, where do you want to go?"

The Princesse was on the verge of tears, and her lower lip was quivering. "To France," was all she could answer.

"Be yourself, sister," said the man, with a touch of impatience in his voice.

Two officers of the law emerged from an alley at this moment. One of them approached the car in a desultory way and said, "What's all this to-do?" Taking a pencil in hand, he bade the Princesse give him her name in full.

"In *full?*" she inquired. He nodded. Gasping for breath, she obeyed. "I am Princesse Valentine Amélie Cathérine Aurélie Thérèse Louise Françoise Angèle de Villefranche."

"Sez you," said the officer.

The second officer, having noticed the pink-sweatered corpse which completely concealed young Almont's body, nudged his companion. "Let 'em alone—it's a gangster killing. Good riddance of bad rubbish. An Indigo has bumped off a Pink. It's just a public blessing."

"O.K. Bud," the first officer said, and they both returned to the alley. As they left they resumed their interrupted conversation, and the Princesse heard one saying, as his voice trailed away in the distance, "Well, you may be right, but I prefer Marlene. What I never liked about Greta is that her arms are so bloomin' long."

The young man in the blue sweater was regarding the Princesse now with an intense new interest. "Did you say you were a Princesse?" he faced her incredulously.

"Yes."

"And what did you say about Villefranche?"

"That is my seat—my ancient family seat."

"You mean you live in France and everything?"

"Yes." The Princesse submitted graciously to this species of questionnaire because the young man seemed sincerely interested.

"Do you have any pull in the ports over there?"

"Any *pull?*" She was again nonplussed.

"I mean, do you know any High Moguls who would

wink at whatever you did?"

The Princesse did not understand, but she said, "I know all the Faubourg Saint-Germain."

"Boy, what a break for all of us! Watch me step on it," the young man said as he started the car around a corner.

"Please take me to my hotel," the Princesse muttered, feeling faint and exhausted.

"No sir, sister! You're coming with me to Gang head-quarters."

The word "Gang" struck the Princesse's consciousness like a quick death-dealing thunderbolt. Until then she had not been clearly convinced that she was in the clutches of Gangdom. The shootings had been terrifying to be sure, but they had seemed unreal to the Princesse. She had never been in the presence of shooting before, and it all seemed pretty fictitious. But *Gang!* She suddenly recalled the phrase "being taken for a ride." It was well known even in Europe, and she knew that it meant sure death every time for the person who was being taken. "I am being taken for a ride," she reflected, and therewith she fainted away.

When the Princesse fully regained her consciousness several hours later, she regarded her surroundings with surprise. She was lying propped up on a wide brass bed in what seemed to be a cheap hotel room. The fading wallpaper was striped with rigid rows of red carnations. And above a dresser was hung a large framed print of *The Age of Innocence*. At the foot of the bed sat the young man in the blue sweater, solicitously holding Albertine in his lap. He smiled an ingratiating smile which put the Princesse momentarily at ease. Then he called to someone in the connecting room. "Come in, Boss. The Princesse is O.K. now."

Through the door there came a corpulent middle-aged man in a blue silk sweater. He was followed by a slight companion who was dressed in a blue cotton sweater.

"Don't be afraid," the big man said. "We are not gorillas."

"I did not think you were," the Princesse replied politely.

The young man who had brought the Princesse to her mystifying retreat negotiated now the introductions. "Princesse, this is Angelo Dogenardi, better known as Little Doggie. He's the Big Shot. And behind him is Bantam Luna, who is the Little Shot. Let me introduce myself too, Princesse. I'm Jimmy Piacere. I'm the Medium Sized Shot."

His manner was so polite, and the introductions were so much more ceremonious than many she had experienced at social events in New York, that the Princesse assumed her most correct manner. *"Messieurs, je suis enchantée,"* she said courteously.

The Princesse felt no fright, but still she wondered where she was. Jimmy Piacere sensed her wonderment and explained her present surroundings. She was in the Liberty Hotel in a suburb of Detroit. The hotel, he revealed, was the headquarters of his pals, the Indigo Gang. They were a gang of bootleggers who had specialized in rum-running on the Canadian border. But recently the Pink Gang had

(236)

been muscling in on their business. The Indigo Gang was now contemplating leaving Detroit, and engaging in a transatlantic business.

"Those Pinks are tough birds, sister," Jimmy Piacere concluded. "We'd call a truce, but they won't talk turkey."

"You see," said Little Doggie, "we want to get out from under. We're sick of the sound of typewriters. We're gonna get ourselves another milk-route."

The Princesse inferred nothing but looked sympathetic.

Jimmy Piacere looked tearful. "That Pink I got to-day sort of evens things up for Little Dick. My little kid brother was an awful rotter, but Jeez, I loved him, Princesse."

"Did I understand rightly that the rats got your brother?" the Princesse anxiously asked.

"*You* tell the cockeyed world!" said Jimmy Piacere.

"Fancy!" exclaimed the Princesse. The telephone rang, interrupting her amazement. Bantam Luna went to answer it and returned with the news that the Cockroach was on the wire. Little Doggie went to speak to him, and Jimmy Piacere explained to the Princesse that the Cockroach was one Cock Robbins who was known as the Roasting Ears King. He collected tribute as a corn racketeer throughout the Middle West, and was now collecting from bootleggers as well as from farmers on the ground that corn was used in making whisky.

"The Cockroach is coming up," said Little Doggie. A moment later the gentleman was ushered into the room, and once again Jimmy Piacere effected an introduction of the

Princesse. She shook hands with the Cockroach, and he turned at once to his business. "Got a C for me?" he menaced Little Doggie.

Silently the Big Shot removed a hundred dollar bill from the pages of a Gideon Bible. He pressed it into the racketeer's hand, and the Roasting Ears King departed.

Little Doggie looked crestfallen. "I'm the goat," he said.

"It's really very odd, the way he talks about the animals," the Princesse reflected. "He says he's the goat, and that he's not a gorilla. It's probably something Freudian," she dismissed the subject.

"Princesse," said Little Doggie, "you probably wonder why we have brought you here. To come to the point, we want to make you a business proposition. Won't you come along in to supper where we can talk things over?"

The Princesse felt famished and was delighted by the mention of supper. Little Doggie led the way through several connecting rooms. He plodded along with a leisurely waddle because of his excess weight. (He had acquired the name "Little Doggie" in the days antedating his corpulence.) At length they were in a dining room where a table was set for four. In one corner of the room the Princesse seemed to discern the Cathedral of Milano. She assumed that this was an optical illusion, but coming nearer she found that she was looking at a cake. It rose from the floor as high as her head, and was covered with glittering frosting.

"That's left over from a banquet we had last night,"

Little Doggie explained to the Princesse. "We ate the back of the Duomo first, so as to save the façade as long as possible. We'll eat the façade to-night," he added, waving the Princesse into her chair. Once seated at the table, Little Doggie became suddenly executive. "Now Princesse, we've got a plan to get you in the bucks. I suppose even though you're a Princesse you could do with some extra cash."

"*Bien sur,*" the Princesse was open-minded.

"Well, here's the plan. Villefranche is a port town with a swell little harbor, isn't it?"

"Oh yes," replied the Princesse. "My house there is on the water's edge, and boats come right up near it."

"Just what I hoped," smiled Little Doggie. "Now if a boat, say a private yacht, was loaded there I suppose no authorities would interfere?"

"Why no," exclaimed the Princesse. "Authorities never molest the yachts of my friends when they anchor there."

Little Doggie then concisely presented his project. His gang had been contemplating establishing a base in the South of France and smuggling liquor from there across to the Bahamas and into Florida. Villefranche would serve as an ideal port, and if the Princesse would consent to hook up with the gang, and shield them from interference by local port authorities, they would all be sitting pretty, said Little Doggie. The Indigo Gang had recently purchased a yacht which would cross the Atlantic in two weeks. It was ready to sail from Jersey City, and the Princesse might return to France on it, Little Doggie suggested.

The Princesse was overjoyed by this suggestion. To cross the Atlantic in a yacht would be delightful. And these men were so polite and kind-hearted that she would enjoy associating with them. They had been so kind to Albertine, it was plain that they were gentlemen. Besides, what a gratification to make some money! The Princesse's trip to America had cut a considerable hole in her accessible funds. "I had planned to return to France in about two weeks," she addressed Little Doggie.

"The *Ritorna Vincitor* can sail any time you say," the Big Shot informed her. A round of red wine was poured, and then the cake-cathedral was cut.

"Just a small piece for me," said the Princesse. "I'd like just a bit of a buttress."

An hilarious toast was drunk, and the Princess then asked to be excused for the night. Jimmy Piacere escorted her downstairs into the lobby of the Liberty Hotel. Quite a lot of brown women were standing about waiting to get their keys. Jimmy Piacere explained that they were members of a convention of Mulatto Gold Star Mothers who were obliged to convene in the suburbs because the smart hotels had not welcomed them.

Arriving at her own hotel, the Princesse found things in an uproar. All the loungers in the lobby were feverishly devouring night editions of the local papers. Streaming headlines on every page referred to The April Fool's Day Massacre. The Princesse felt a certain pride in the realization that she had participated in it. Such an adventure gave her American trip a semblance of a climax. And her book of Impressions could end now on an authentically exciting note.

The hotel desk clerk called her attention to a paragraph in a front page story:

"The killers were not apprehended. Police report that a woman was seen in the death car belonging to Jasper Almont, and that she claimed to be the Princesse de Villefranche. At the time the officer believed this name to be fictitious. It has been learned however that the Princesse did leave the Hotel Aquoisert with young Almont about three hours before the killings and has not been heard from since. It is believed that she has been kidnaped by the killers. Grave alarm is felt that she may be in the hands of Angelo Little Doggie Dogenardi, the Indigo chief whose gang is suspected of perpetrating the crime. Pedestrians in the vicinity of the massacre say they identified Jimmy Boo-Hoo Piacere and Bantam Con Amore Luna as the death car raced toward Jefferson Avenue followed by another car."

"Now that you've returned safe and sound," said the clerk, "won't you give out a statement for the press?"

The Princess realized that she must say nothing which would jeopardize her new associates, and she tried to think

up something non-committal. "Just say that they were horrible men and they tried to steal my cat. They took me for
a ride to frighten me, and then they made me walk back."
She felt quite satisfied with this statement which seemed to
her to cover all the ground.

Worn out but feeling jubilant, the Princesse went to bed
immediately. Before going to sleep she glanced through her
mail which the hysterical Mirabelle brought her. A note
from the firm of Oiseau in Paris made the Princesse's heart
sink in despair. The firm, it formally informed her, would
be unable to publish her book. The sample chapters which
she had submitted had been read and finally rejected. The
things she described were too implausible, and nobody in
France would believe them. The firm of Oiseau deplored
this verdict, and was hers respectfully and devotedly and
she could believe in its best and friendliest and most distinguished sentiments.

"But everything I wrote was *true*," wailed the Princesse,
bursting into tears. She was so overcome that she sank at
once into broken-hearted sleep.

Next day at noon she awoke and found Mirabelle almost
lost in telegrams. Innumerable messages had arrived from
friends who had learned that the Princesse was safe. Many
communications were not from friends, and the Princesse
was bewildered. All sorts of editors were begging for her
story of the April Fool's Day Massacre. A vaudeville
agency offered her a six weeks engagement in and around

New York. Chicago dailies requested her to telephone her photograph at once. A night letter importuned her to act as a patroness at the gala opening of the Television Exposition in New York the following week. Best of all, a wire from Wilburton Renegade stated that he had heard that the Princesse was writing a book of American Impressions. If the rights were not tied up with the French firm, he would like to publish the book in English. The Princesse overnight had become a "big name" and would be a "big seller," he advised her.

"We must pack and go back to New York at once," she excitedly told Mirabelle.

And that night the Princesse was on her way east, traveling incognito in a compartment. She was eagerly putting down the facts relating to her experience with the gangsters —omitting of course all reference to her future association with them. Her pen shaking with the motion of the car, she wrote: "A very surprising plague of rats, I was told, killed a number of these men last year. The rats seemed to concentrate exclusively on the younger brothers of the gangmen, in the manner of ancient Biblical plagues in Egypt. This may—who knows?—be an omen from On High."

When her hand became tired the Princesse settled down in her pillows and looked out on the moonlit wastes of Canada. "I suppose, if people knew, they would call me a *bootlegger*," she reflected. The word had a common air about it. What would it be in French? The Princesse pondered. Someone—was it Paul Morand?—had translated *speakeasy* literally into French as *cause-en-douce*. She might do the same for *bootlegger,* the Princesse mused. Boot was *botte* and leg was *jambe,* and the Princesse juxtaposed them. "I'm a *bottejambière*," she said to herself as the train rolled over Ontario.

XVI

The "April Fool's Day Massacre" became an international scandal. The indignation of two continents was aroused by the inhuman aspects of the killing. Very little attention was paid to the human aspects of the dying.

The French Republic made official complaint against the alleged attack on one of its Princesses. And the entire American press devoted columns to the episode. Some editorials proclaimed that even if the Princesse *had* been smuggling liquor the shooting would still be unjustified. Other editorials took the attitude that the killing of Jasper Almont was fairly authorized; that the loss of a cat would be little to suffer if the Princesse were under suspicion; and that visiting titled foreigners would have to learn to comply to American laws, particularly foreign visitors who were used to the laxity of New York.

Middle Western editorials harped on the fact that life in New York was corrupt. "Dry" editors made an investigation of the Princesse's winter in the metropolis, and gleefully reminded the public that she had been "mixed up" in the "orgy" at Lenore Lanslide's, where forty guests, as the paper put it, had "drunk themselves to death." Furthermore, conservative editors pointed out, she was a friend of Aurora Overauhl who was well known to be a monarchist, and who was rumored to be plotting against the interests of American Democracy. In the end it was even alleged that the Princesse's visit to Detroit was part of a Royalist plot. The journalistic war waxed more and more violent, and public opinion grew to be more heated than it had been since the days of the War.

When the Princesse returned to New York, Aurora immediately offered her the hospitality of the gas tank, and its protection against the onslaught of publicity which she knew the poor Princesse would be helpless to ward off in an apartment hotel. But as soon as the Princesse had moved into the tank Aurora began to receive innumerable threatening letters. She was called "a seditious influence" and accused of being "a thinker." She was warned that any night she might expect a bomb to drop on her gas tank. She was advised that the very fact that she lived in a gas tank marked her definitely as "a dangerous freak"; and that her harboring of the Princesse, who was clearly an adventuress, was a brazen manifestation of snobbishness and treason. She was told to take her high hat off and live the way other folks lived.

Aurora debated whether or not to move out of the gas tank. The warnings might be only the documents of cranks;

then again they might be serious. She was still debating when an unforeseen development forced her decision. She was informed by her realty agents that the gas tank (which she had rented on a short term lease) had been sold to a big corporation which was buying up gas tanks across the country with a novel aim in view. The tanks were to be filled not with gas but with liquor, and in turn would supply filling stations. Motor cars would be supplied with false containers into which not gas but Scotch would pour. The corporation was in fact the opulent Pink Gang whose leaders were prompted to these extreme measures by their fear that the picturesque "dry" era was about to end and that quick intensive profit taking was in order.

Aurora was immeasurably depressed by her predicament, though less by her personal predicament than by the predicament of her country, her hapless, rudderless country which she knew she now must leave. Her life had become impossible in a land where her last resource, her privacy, was invaded and treated as an unpardonable eccentricity.

In some ways she was loath to leave, for she loved certain aspects of New York. In the present status of the world it was probably her favorite city. Its life was fantastic beyond that of Bagdad. It was a city of lunar paradox, where distinguished Princesses went out casually with Flea Circus freaks, and where impoverished young Englishmen rose into opulence on their looks and their accidental knowledge; a metropolis where everything was topsy-turvy, vulgar and purposeless, grandiose and mad. And New York was living its life, such as it was, in its immediate living present. It was not, as other world cities were, being nourished by the dust of its past. It had, unquestionably, many facts in its favor. But, amusing and exciting as it was, Aurora aspired to a loftier dwelling place. She had reached the saturation point of amusement and excitement, and she needed to find an habitat where her spirit might take root. She was not in accord with the times in New York, and the question was where to go.

The Princesse offered Aurora the use of her apartment in Paris. And Aurora carefully thought the matter over. Should she go to Paris, which, contrary to popular legend, was really a city to weep in, a city where former glory had given way to gray reminiscence? Should Aurora go to Paris and dress up as Carthage in costume balls at the Duquesa Barocca's? Perish the thought! Should she play around with sailors in *boîtes*? Or frequent the salon of the Comtesse de Contrecoeur and discuss the merits of Rimbaud? Or haunt the Ritz Bar, drinking champagne cocktails with lost American divorcees? Should she settle in Montparnasse and excite herself over the manifesto of some new *isme*? And applaud the *Sur-Réaliste* films of cows on lace couches and reindeer in grand pianos? Aurora felt some sympathy with the creators of these films. She realized that in "art" there was little left to do save to stuff reindeer into grand pianos. But the sad young men could negotiate this without her participation. Why should she go to Paris to exchange one form of death for another?

Aurora lighted a cigarette, and let her mind's eye roam over the world. Should she go to Italy, where an aggressive industrialism was speeding up the traffic on the sad canals of Venice? Or, eschewing Fascist Italy, should she retreat to Siena, Fiesole, or such dusty museum towns? They were beautiful places to die in, but Aurora sought a place to live in. She felt no nostalgia for the good old days. Her nostalgia was all for the good new days which she found nowhere in sight.

Should she investigate Soviet Russia, a land where the Fordson tractor had become the symbol of heart's desire? No, she decided.

Taking leave of Civilization, should she retreat to the depths of the country and cultivate her garden? This Voltairean solution was practicable, she concluded, only if gardening had been an exclusive life-long pursuit.

She must leave New York immediately, and what was the best Earth had to offer to her ripe, discriminating mind? Which way lay release from the encircling mediocrity, from the increasing impact of standardized, sterilized vulgarity? Where did there exist a shred of national, international, or individual pure nobility of purpose?

Before making any definite decision she consented to go with the Princesse to the opening night of the Television Exposition. Television was an uncharted wonder which she felt she ought to investigate. Its promoters promised no end of miracles on the opening night of the Exposition. Experiments which scientists had been working on in secret were

now perfected and ready for public demonstration. Trans-
Atlantic Television was a reality at last. The world was
entering a new era.

The Exposition was being held in the Television Center,
a low, modernistic construction of aluminum and glass, severely geometrical in design, and wholly flimsy in effect.
The Demonstration Room was a large hall with pigskin
walls adorned with a few scrappy murals of inlaid linoleum.
It was filled with four hundred barber chairs to accommodate the guests at the exclusive opening night. These chairs
had been a last minute solution of a very troublesome problem. All the most advanced decorators had submitted designs of modernistic chairs for this room. But all the designs
had been so prohibitively expensive to execute, and they
were all so similar and so much like barber chairs in princi-
ple (leather and chrome-plated steel), that the executives
in charge of the project had finally settled upon just using
barber chairs and being done with it.

Aurora Overauhl and the Princesse entered the room and
found it crowded with all the same people who were asked
to all first nights in New York. An announcer was making
a speech in praise of the imminent revelations. No longer,
he said, would newsreels show news of the world a week
or a day late. Beginning to-night world events could be seen
and heard as they actually transpired. To-night this privileged group would be present at representative activities all
over the earth. Aurora settled into her barber chair and
hoped, oh desperately, for some sign that would point her

way to a new destination.

The lights in the hall were lowered and the image receiver lighted up. A bell struck the hour, and suddenly one
saw the Spring Fête of the Duquesa Barocca! It was taking
place in the catacombs of Rome which she had chartered
for a day as a whim. It was called the Fête of the Beverages,
and the Duquesa herself, completely concealed in a coil of
colored cellophane, was standing inside a huge crystal bottle
emblazoned with the letters MUMM. A concealed orchestra
was softly playing *Why Did You Have to Go?*

"Fancy!" cried the Princesse. She could say no more.
Aurora said nothing at all.

Then followed in quick succession a series of shots from
the ends of the earth, all carefully timed for the hook-up.
There was the opening of the Club Lizard Loins in Chicago
where Gala Bumpus was acting as hostess and Racy was
doing his specialty dance to *Why Did You Have to Go?*
There was a public demonstration in a plaza in Buenos Aires
at the unveiling of Lenore Lanslide's monument. There was
a reception scene in the palace of the King of Trans-Urania
following the wedding of the Van Dongen twins and
Napier Knightsbridge. The twins made a brief bashful
speech and declared they were the happiest couple in the
world. The scene then switched to Bavaria, to a *Freilichtpark*
of the Nudists.

"Oh!" cried the Princesse. "*C'est trop fort!* I see Aimée
de Vaugirard!" But before she could point her out to
Aurora the scene had faded into obscurity by sudden order

of an international censor.

The receiver lighted up again to show the terrace of a luxurious Palm Beach hotel, where Armada Menace-Renegade in a moonlit setting was singing the aria from *Mignon:*

> *"Connais-tu le pays*
> *Ou fleurit l'oranger?"*

When she had finished a gentleman took her place in the center of the picture and remarked, "Ladies and gentlemen, just give a thought to the opening lines of that song: *Dost thou know yonder land where the orange grows?* Surely the Poet had Florida in mind—Florida, the Empire of the Sun! Now, our corporation is developing the Everglades and—"

Niobe Why fled the hall at this moment crying "Ballyhoo! Ballyhoo! Ballyhoo! It's even worse than the Radio. Ballyhoo! Ballyhoo! Ballyhoo!" Many people feared she had gone insane, but her friends were accustomed to these exits and paid no attention to her departure.

The next scene was in Majorca where Pamela Woodley-Knightsbridge was standing beside the sea with a black cigar in her mouth. She was made up for her first co-starring rôle in a film entitled *Bad Girl of Paris*. It was a dramatization of the Chopin episode in the life of George Sand, and the Majorcan sequences were being shot in the actual scenes of the romance. Robert Reindeer was appearing as Chopin, and was working in this film and in *The Bible in Spain* simultaneously, thus doing strenuous double duty while on location in and about Spain.

Pamela faced her audience in New York and said, "It gives me great pleasure to introduce Robert Reindeer who will now hold a conversation with Miss April Overjoy in Hollywood. They are thousands of miles apart, but you can see them and hear them speaking in the most epochal conversation that the world has ever known."

"Hello, April," said Robert Reindeer.

"Hello, Robert," said April Overjoy.

"Isn't it wonderful?" said Robert.

"Wonderful, isn't it?" said April.

"Just think of us being able to talk like this."

"It's wonderful," said April, and the talk was over.

"My friends," said Pamela Woodley-Knightsbridge, "you have just heard two of the world's most famous and best loved people in the most world-rocking conversation the world has ever known."

Aurora Overauhl sighed. She had arrived at the depressing realization that a concomitant of the perfection of facilities for communication was the fact that no one had anything to communicate.

The final sequence was beginning. A world conference on Disarmament was being held somewhere in Switzerland. The representatives of all the civilized nations were sitting around a table. Due to the Alpine atmospheric conditions the images were hazy and it was impossible to distinguish clearly the different speakers. But one was heard to be saying, "Well, we'll abolish bombing planes if you'll abolish battleships over 10,000 tons."

"We won't abolish anything unless you abolish poison gas."

"But if we abolish poison gas our frontiers will be unprotected, and we'll have to be permitted submarines."

"If you are permitted submarines," said a third nation, "then we demand that they be below a 150-ton limit."

"Not unless you scrap your tanks."

"We refuse to scrap our whippet tanks that weigh less than 20 tons."

"Then we won't abolish bombing planes at all," said the first nation. And it all began over again, and went on and on all night. For some reason the mechanicians could not stop the unfamiliar apparatus. And as the members of the audience were all invited guests they felt it would be rude to leave. It was almost dawn when the conference closed on the point where it had begun.

The announcer then announced that the entire night's program had been photographed and recorded, and that to-morrow the records would be broadcast over Station PGPG. From now on no word ever spoken would ever need to be lost. As the awe-stricken guests dispersed in the street a loud speaker was replaying a recording of *Why Did You Have to Go?* as played at the Duquesa's Fête in the catacombs.

Aurora listened sadly. The words were suddenly *à propos*. Why *did* she have to go? There had been nothing in the Television program of representative world events to persuade her that life was any more admirable one place than another. Indeed, every place had become so accessible that all places were now the same place. There were no un-contaminated regions on earth. Not on the entire planet. Aurora looked up at the stars which were fading with the slow approach of the dawn. Then and there she made a sudden joyous discovery. There were still the other planets!

The Princesse was excited by the events of the night and wanted to sit up and discuss them. But Aurora plead fatigue, and the Princesse went reluctantly to bed. Then Aurora changed into her flying clothes and silently climbed out of the gas tank.

"What you up to?" asked old Meraude who was always awake bright and early.

"I'm going somewhere," Aurora replied, making a brisk take-off.

Old Meraude with her failing sight could scarcely focus the plane in its flight. When she saw it last it seemed to be soaring straight toward the sun at dawn.

Three days later Aurora had not been heard from. Three weeks later she was given up as "lost." Her friends were all grief-stricken and Angèle de Villefranche was panicky. The Princesse was making muddled preparations to sail on the Indigo Gang's yacht. She had sold her book to the Renegade firm by way of Robespierre Lanslide. The literary agent had approached her as soon as she arrived in New

York, and had importuned her to let him sell her book to Renegade.

"But I don't need an agent," the Princesse protested. "I know Mr. Renegade myself."

But the agent had insisted that he could get her better terms. So she put the matter into his hands, and in the end she had signed a contract by which her agent received more money for selling the book than she would ever receive in royalties from its sale.

Niobe Why, a stricken woman, was going to sail on the yacht with the Princesse. She had come to America to clip her coupons, but had found that none of her securities were sound, and that none of her coupons could be redeemed. She had been "wiped out" without knowing how, and her friends all said, "Poor soul." She would not have been able to return to France had it not been for the kindness of the Princesse.

Clarissa Goode saw the Princesse and Mrs. Why off to France one rainy afternoon in May. The yacht, the *Ritorna Vincitor,* was moored at a pier in Jersey City. And Jimmy Piacere, dressed up as a skipper, was nervous and impatient to embark.

Niobe Why stood at the end of the gangplank and gloomily wiped her eyes. "These tears are not for myself," she said. "I'm shedding them for Aurora."

"Brace up, Niobe," said Clarissa Goode. "Aurora may still be heard from. You know she wouldn't kill herself. She's far too brave to do that."

"I know," sobbed Niobe Why.

"And I don't believe she had an accident either," Clarissa Goode continued. "She liked to pretend she was a bad mechanic, but she really was a pretty damned good one."

"I know," whispered Niobe Why.

"Old Meraude insists that the plane could not have gone far on the gas that was in it. Aurora is probably just hiding somewhere because she's tired of it all." Clarissa Goode, as always, was sniffing after the best.

But Niobe Why would not permit herself the satisfaction of comfort. "Ah no," she said, "Aurora would not keep her friends in suspense like that."

Clarissa Goode was growing belligerent. "Since you take such pleasure in your grief," she said, "I won't disturb it further. I see you're determined to have Aurora dead."

"No I'm not," Mrs. Why protested. "How can you say such a thing?" She then in broken accents put forth her own explanation. "I think her disappearance points a return to the age of miracles. I honestly believe," said Niobe Why, "that Aurora has ascended into Heaven."

The Princesse looked as though all things were equally beyond her. She waved her handkerchief wildly as the gangplank was withdrawn. Then, assuming her most authoritative manner, she summoned Jimmy Piacere. "To Villefranche, James," she said.